SWITCH BITCH

A grieving widow, slowly beginning to inch back into the land of the living, reaches out to an old flame — an act which will have dramatic consequences. Two husbands concoct a plan to bring excitement back into their marital beds: swapping wives for the night — but without the women's knowledge. And extracts from the personal diaries of the libidinous Oswald Hendryks Cornelius are published for the first time: detailing his experiences with a violently aphrodisiac perfume; and how, stranded in the desert, he is taken in by a mother and daughter — who offer considerably more hospitality than he'd bargained for . . .

Books by Roald Dahl
Published in Ulverscroft Collections:

KISS KISS
SOMEONE LIKE YOU
THE WONDERFUL STORY OF
HENRY SUGAR

ROALD DAHL

♦

SWITCH BITCH
Tales of the Unexpected

Complete and Unabridged

ULVERSCROFT
Leicester

First published in Great Britain in 1974 by
Michael Joseph
London

This Ulverscroft Edition
published 2019
by arrangement with
David Higham Associates Literary Agency
London

A catalogue record for this book is available
from the British Library.

ISBN 978–1–4448–3951–7

Published by
F. A. Thorpe (Publishing)
Anstey, Leicestershire

Set by Words & Graphics Ltd.
Anstey, Leicestershire
Printed and bound in Great Britain by
T. J. International Ltd., Padstow, Cornwall

This book is printed on acid-free paper

Contents

The Visitor

Not long ago, a large wooden case was deposited at the door of my house by the railway delivery service. It was an unusually strong and well-constructed object, and made of some kind of dark-red hardwood, not unlike mahogany. I lifted it with great difficulty on to a table in the garden, and examined it carefully. The stencilling on one side said that it had been shipped from Haifa by the m/v *Waverley Star*, but I could find no sender's name or address. I tried to think of somebody living in Haifa or thereabouts who might be wanting to send me a magnificent present. I could think of no one. I walked slowly to the toolshed, still pondering the matter deeply, and returned with a hammer and screwdriver. Then I began gently to prise open the top of the case.

Behold, it was filled with books! Extraordinary books! One by one, I lifted them all out (not yet looking inside any of them) and stacked them in three tall piles on the table. There were twenty-eight volumes altogether, and very beautiful they were indeed. Each of them was identically and superbly bound in rich green morocco, with the initials O.H.C. and a Roman numeral (I to XXVIII) tooled in gold upon the spine.

I took up the nearest volume, number XVI, and opened it. The unlined white pages were filled with a neat small handwriting in black ink. On the title page was written '1934'. Nothing

1

else. I took up another volume, number XXI. It contained more manuscript in the same handwriting, but on the title page it said '1939'. I put it down and pulled out volume I, hoping to find a preface of some kind there, or perhaps the author's name. Instead, I found an envelope inside the cover. The envelope was addressed to me. I took out the letter it contained and glanced quickly at the signature. *Oswald Hendryks Cornelius*, it said.

It was Uncle Oswald!

No member of the family had heard from Uncle Oswald for over thirty years. This letter was dated 10 March 1964, and until its arrival, we could only assume that he still existed. Nothing was really known about him except that he lived in France, that he travelled a great deal, that he was a wealthy bachelor with unsavoury but glamorous habits who steadfastly refused to have anything to do with his own relatives. The rest was all rumour and hearsay, but the rumours were so splendid and the hearsay so exotic that Oswald had long since become a shining hero and a legend to us all.

'My dear boy,' the letter began,

I believe that you and your three sisters are my closest surviving blood relations. You are therefore my rightful heirs, and because I have made no will, all that I leave behind me when I die will be yours. Alas, I have nothing to leave. I used to have quite a lot, and the fact that I have recently disposed of it all in my own way is none of your

2

business. As consolation, though, I am sending you my private diaries. These, I think, ought to remain in the family. They cover all the best years of my life, and it will do you no harm to read them. But if you show them around or lend them to strangers, you do so at your own great peril. If you publish them, then that, I should imagine, would be the end of both you and your publisher simultaneously. For you must understand that thousands of the heroines whom I mention in the diaries are still only half dead, and if you were foolish enough to splash their lily white reputation with scarlet print, they would have your head on a salver in two seconds flat, and probably roast it in the oven for good measure. So you'd better be careful. I only met you once. That was years ago, in 1921, when your family was living in that large ugly house in South Wales. I was your big uncle and you were a very small boy, about five years old. I don't suppose you remember the young Norwegian nursemaid you had then. A remarkably clean, well-built girl she was, and exquisitely shaped even in her uniform with its ridiculously starchy white shield concealing her lovely bosom. The afternoon I was there, she was taking you for a walk in the woods to pick bluebells, and I asked if I might come along. And when we got well into the middle of the woods, I told you I'd give you a bar of chocolate if

you could find your own way home. And
you did (see Vol. III). You were a sensible
child. Farewell — Oswald Hendryks Cor-
nelius.

The sudden arrival of the diaries caused much excitement in the family, and there was a rush to read them. We were not disappointed. It was astonishing stuff — hilarious, witty, exciting, and often quite touching as well. The man's vitality was unbelievable. He was always on the move, from city to city, from country to country, from woman to woman, and in between the women, he would be searching for spiders in Kashmir or tracking down a blue porcelain vase in Nanking. But the women always came first. Wherever he went, he left an endless trail of females in his wake, females ruffled and ravished beyond words, but purring like cats.

Twenty-eight volumes with exactly three hundred pages to each volume takes a deal of reading, and there are precious few writers who could hold an audience over a distance like that. But Oswald did it. The narrative never seemed to lose its flavour, the pace seldom slackened, and almost without exception, every single entry, whether it was long or short, and whatever the subject, became a marvellous little individual story that was complete in itself. And at the end of it all, when the last page of the last volume had been read, one was left with the rather breathless feeling that this might just possibly be one of the major autobiographical works of our time.

If it were regarded solely as a chronicle of a man's amorous adventures, then without a doubt there was nothing to touch it. Casanova's *Memoirs* read like a Parish Magazine in comparison, and the famous lover himself, beside Oswald, appears positively undersexed.

There was social dynamite on every page; Oswald was right about that. But he was surely wrong in thinking that the explosions would all come from the women. What about their husbands, the humiliated cock-sparrows, the cuckolds? The cuckold, when aroused, is a very fierce bird indeed, and there would be thousands upon thousands of them rising up out of the bushes if The Cornelius Diaries, unabridged, saw the light of day while they were still alive. Publication, therefore, was right out of the question.

A pity, this. Such a pity, in fact, that I thought something ought to be done about it. So I sat down and re-read the diaries from beginning to end in the hope that I might discover at least one complete passage which could be printed and published without involving both the publisher and myself in serious litigation. To my joy, I found no less than six. I showed them to a lawyer. He said he thought they *might* be 'safe', but he wouldn't guarantee it. One of them — The Sinai Desert Episode — seemed 'safer' than the other five, he added.

So I have decided to start with that one and to offer it for publication right away, at the end of this short preface. If it is accepted and all goes well, then perhaps I shall release one or two more.

The Sinai entry is from the last volume of all, Vol. XXVIII, and is dated 24 August 1946. In point of fact, it is the *very last entry* of the last volume of all, the last thing Oswald ever wrote, and we have no record of where he went or what he did after that date. One can only guess. You shall have the entry verbatim in a moment, but first of all, and so that you may more easily understand some of the things Oswald says and does in his story, let me try to tell you a little about the man himself. Out of the mass of confession and opinion contained in those twenty-eight volumes, there emerges a fairly clear picture of his character.

At the time of the Sinai episode, Oswald Hendryks Cornelius was fifty-one years old, and he had, of course, never been married. 'I am afraid,' he was in the habit of saying, 'that I have been blessed or should I call it burdened, with an uncommonly fastidious nature.'

In some ways, this was true, but in others, and especially in so far as marriage was concerned, the statement was the exact opposite of the truth.

The real reason Oswald had refused to get married was simply that he had never in his life been able to confine his attentions to one particular woman for longer than the time it took to conquer her. When that was done, he lost interest and looked around for another victim.

A normal man would hardly consider this a valid reason for remaining single, but Oswald was not a normal man. He was not even a normal polygamous man. He was, to be honest, such a wanton and incorrigible philanderer that no bride on earth would have put up with him for more than a few days, let alone for the duration of a honeymoon — although heaven knows there were enough who would have been willing to give it a try.

He was a tall, narrow person with a fragile and faintly aesthetic air. His voice was soft, his manner was courteous, and at first sight he seemed more like a gentleman-in-waiting to the queen than a celebrated rapscallion. He never discussed his amorous affairs with other men, and a stranger, though he sit and talk with him all evening, would be unable to observe the slightest sign of deceit in Oswald's clear blue eyes. He was, in fact, precisely the sort of man that an anxious father would be likely to choose to escort his daughter safely home.

But sit Oswald beside a *woman*, a woman who interested him, and instantaneously his eyes would change, and as he looked at her, a small dangerous spark would begin dancing slowly in the very centre of each pupil; and then he would set about her with his conversation, talking to her rapidly and cleverly and almost certainly more wittily than anyone else had ever done before. This was a gift he had, a most singular talent, and when he put his mind to it, he could make his words coil themselves around and around the listener until they held her in some sort of a mild hypnotic spell.

But it wasn't only his fine talk and the look in his eyes that fascinated the women. It was also his nose. (In Vol. XIV, Oswald includes, with obvious relish, a note written to him by a certain lady in which she describes such things as this in great detail.) It appears that when Oswald was aroused, something odd would begin to happen around the edges of his nostrils, a tightening of the rims, a visible flaring which enlarged the nostril holes and revealed whole areas of the bright red skin inside. This created a queer, wild, animalistic impression, and although it may not sound particularly attractive when described on paper, its effect upon the ladies was electric.

Almost without exception, women were drawn toward Oswald. In the first place, he was a man who refused to be owned at any price, and this automatically made him desirable. Add to this the unusual combination of a first-rate intellect, an abundance of charm, and a reputation for excessive promiscuity, and you have a potent recipe.

Then again, and forgetting for a moment the disreputable and licentious angle, it should be noted that there were a number of other surprising facets to Oswald's character that in themselves made him a rather intriguing person. There was, for example, very little that he did not know about nineteenth-century Italian opera, and he had written a curious little manual upon the three composers Donizetti, Verdi, and Ponchielli. In it, he listed by name all the important mistresses that these men had had during their lives, and he went on to examine, in a most serious vein, the relationship between creative passion and carnal passion, and the influence of the one upon the other, particularly as it affected the works of these composers.

Chinese porcelain was another of Oswald's interests, and he was acknowledged as something of an international authority in this field. The blue vases of the Tchin-Hoa period were his special love, and he had a small but exquisite collection of these pieces.

He also collected spiders and walking sticks.

His collection of spiders, or more accurately his collection of Arachnida, because it included scorpions and pedipalps, was possibly as comprehensive as any outside a museum, and his knowledge of the hundreds of genera and species was impressive. He maintained, incidentally (and probably correctly), that the spider's silk was superior in quality to the ordinary stuff spun by silkworms, and he never wore a tie that was made of any other material. He possessed about forty of these ties altogether, and in order to acquire them in the first place, and in order also to be able to add two new ties a year to his wardrobe, he had to keep thousands and thousands of *Arana* and *Epeira diademata* (the common English garden spiders) in an old conservatory in the garden of his country house outside Paris, where they bred and multiplied at approximately the same rate as they ate one another. From them, he collected the raw thread himself — no one else would enter that ghastly glasshouse — and sent it to Avignon, where it was reeled and thrown and scoured and dyed and made into cloth. From Avignon, the cloth was delivered directly to Sulka, who were enchanted by the whole business, and only too glad to fashion ties out of such a rare and wonderful material.

'But you can't *really* like spiders?' the women visitors would say to Oswald as he displayed his collection.

'Oh, but I adore them,' he would answer. 'Especially the females. They remind me so much of certain human females that I know. They remind me of my very favourite human females.'

'What nonsense, darling.'

'Nonsense? I think not.'

'It's rather insulting.'

'On the contrary, my dear, it is the greatest compliment I could pay. Did you not know, for instance, that the female spider is so savage in her lovemaking that the male is very lucky indeed if he escapes with his life at the end of it all. Only if he is exceedingly agile and marvellously ingenious will he get away in one piece.'

'Now, *Oswald!*'

'And the crab spider, my beloved, the teeny-weeny little crab spider is so dangerously passionate that her lover has to tie her down with intricate loops and knots of his own thread before he dares to embrace her . . . '

'Oh, *stop* it, Oswald, this *minute!*' the women would cry, their eyes shining.

Oswald's collection of walking sticks was something else again. Every one of them had belonged either to a distinguished or a disgusting person, and he kept them all in his Paris apartment, where they were displayed in two long racks standing against the walls of the passage (or should one call it the highway?) which led from the living-room to the bedroom. Each stick had its own ivory label above it, saying Sibelius, Milton, King Farouk, Dickens, Robespierre, Puccini, Oscar Wilde, Franklin Roosevelt, Goebbels, Queen Victoria, Toulouse-Lautrec, Hindenburg, Tolstoy, Laval, Sarah Bernhardt, Goethe, Voroshiloff, Cézanne, Toho ... There must have been over a hundred of them in all, some very beautiful, some very plain, some with gold or silver tops, and some with curly handles.

'Take down the Tolstoy,' Oswald would say to a pretty visitor. 'Go on, take it down ... that's right ... and now ... now rub your own palm gently over the knob that has been worn to a shine by the great man himself. Is it not rather wonderful, the mere contact of your skin with that spot?'

'It is, rather, isn't it.'

'And now take the Goebbels and do the same thing. Do it properly, though. Allow your palm to fold tightly over the handle ... good ... and now ... now lean your weight on it, lean hard, exactly as the little deformed doctor used to do ... there ... that's it ... now stay like that for a minute or so and then tell me if you do not feel a thin finger of ice creeping all the way up your arm and into your chest?'

'It's terrifying!'

'Of course it is. Some people pass out completely. They keel right over.'

Nobody ever found it dull to be in Oswald's

11

company, and perhaps that, more than anything else, was the reason for his success.

We come now to the Sinai episode. Oswald, during that month, had been amusing himself by motoring at a fairly leisurely pace down from Khartoum to Cairo. His car was a superlative pre-war Lagonda which had been carefully stored in Switzerland during the war years, and as you can imagine, it was fitted with every kind of gadget under the sun. On the day before Sinai (23 August 1946), he was in Cairo, staying at Shepheard's Hotel, and that evening, after a series of impudent manoeuvres, he had succeeded in getting hold of a Moorish lady of supposedly aristocratic descent, called Isabella. Isabella happened to be the jealously guarded mistress of none other than a certain notorious and dyspeptic Royal Personage (there was still a monarchy in Egypt then). This was a typically Oswaldian move.

But there was more to come. At midnight, he drove the lady out to Giza and persuaded her to climb with him in the moonlight right to the very top of the great pyramid of Cheops.

' . . . There can be no safer place,' he wrote in the diary, 'nor a more romantic one, than the apex of a pyramid on a warm night when the moon is full. The passions are stirred not only by the magnificent view but also by that curious sensation of power that surges within the body whenever one surveys the world from a great height. And as for safety — this pyramid is exactly 481 feet high, which is 115 feet higher than the dome of St Paul's Cathedral, and from the summit one can observe all the approaches with the greatest of ease. No other boudoir on earth can offer this facility. None has so many emergency exits, either, so that if some sinister figure should happen to come clambering up in pursuit on one side of the pyramid, one has only to slip calmly and quietly down the other . . . '

As it happened, Oswald had a very narrow squeak indeed that night. Somehow, the palace must have got word of the little affair, for Oswald, from his lofty moonlit pinnacle, suddenly observed *three* sinister figures, not one, closing in on three different sides, and starting to climb. But luckily for him, there is a fourth side to the great pyramid of Cheops, and by the time those Arab thugs had reached the top, the two lovers were already at the bottom and getting into the car.

The entry for 24 August takes up the story at exactly this point. It is reproduced here word for word and comma for comma as Oswald wrote it. Nothing has been altered or added or taken away:

24 August 1946
'He'll chop off Isabella's head if he catch her now,' Isabella said.

'Rubbish,' I answered, but I reckoned she was probably right.

'He'll chop off Oswald's head, too,' she said.

'Not mine, dear lady. I shall be a long way away from here when daylight comes. I'm heading straight up the Nile for Luxor immediately.'

We were driving quickly away from the pyramids now. It was about two thirty a.m.

13

'To Luxor?' she said.

'Yes.'

'And Isabella is going with you.'

'No,' I said.

'Yes,' she said.

'It is against my principles to travel with a lady,' I said.

I could see some lights ahead of us. They came from the Mena House Hotel, a place where tourists stay out in the desert, not far from the pyramids. I drove fairly close to the hotel and stopped the car.

'I'm going to drop you here,' I said. 'We had a fine time.'

'So you won't take Isabella to Luxor?'

'I'm afraid not,' I said. 'Come on, hop it.'

She started to get out of the car, then she paused with one foot on the road, and suddenly she swung round and poured out upon me a torrent of language so filthy yet so fluent that I had heard nothing like it from the lips of a lady since . . . well, since 1931, in Marrakesh, when the greedy old Duchess of Glasgow put her hand into a chocolate box and got nipped by a scorpion I happened to have placed there for safe-keeping (Vol. XIII, 5 June 1931).

'You are disgusting,' I said.

Isabella leapt out and slammed the door so hard the whole car jumped on its wheels. I drove off very fast. Thank heaven I was rid of her. I cannot abide bad manners in a pretty girl.

As I drove, I kept one eye on the mirror, but as yet no car seemed to be following me. When I came to the outskirts of Cairo, I began threading

14

my way through the side roads, avoiding the centre of the city. I was not particularly worried. The royal watchdogs were unlikely to carry the matter much further. All the same, it would have been foolhardy to go back to Shepheard's at this point. It wasn't necessary, anyway, because all my baggage, except for a small valise, was with me in the car. I never leave suitcases behind me in my room when I go out of an evening in a foreign city. I like to be mobile.

I had no intention, of course, of going to Luxor. I wanted now to get away from Egypt altogether. I didn't like the country at all. Come to think of it, I never had. The place made me feel uncomfortable in my skin. It was the dirtiness of it all, I think, and the putrid smells. But then let us face it, it really is a squalid country, and I have a powerful suspicion, though I hate to say it, that the Egyptians wash themselves less thoroughly than any other peoples in the world — with the possible exception of the Mongolians. Certainly they do not wash their crockery to my taste. There was, believe it or not, a long, crusted, coffee-coloured lipmark stamped upon the rim of the cup they placed before me at breakfast yesterday. Ugh! It was repulsive! I kept staring at it and wondering whose slobbery lower lip had done the deed.

I was driving now through the narrow dirty streets of the eastern suburbs of Cairo. I knew precisely where I was going. I had made up my mind about that before I was even halfway down the pyramid with Isabella. I was going to Jerusalem. It was no distance to speak of, and it was a city that I always enjoyed. Furthermore, it was the quickest way out of Egypt. I would proceed as follows:

1. Cairo to Ismailia. About three hours' driving. Sing an opera on the way, as usual. Arrive Ismailia 6–7 a.m. Take a room and have a two-hour sleep. Then shower, shave, and breakfast.
2. At 10 a.m., cross over the Suez Canal by the Ismailia bridge and take the desert road across Sinai to the Palestine border. Make a search for scorpions *en route* in the Sinai Desert. Time, about four hours, arriving Palestine border 2 p.m.
3. From there, continue straight on to Jerusalem via Beersheba, reaching The King David Hotel in time for cocktails and dinner.

It was several years since I had travelled that particular road, but I remembered that the Sinai Desert was an outstanding place for scorpions. I badly wanted another female opisthophthalmus, a large one. My present specimen had the fifth segment of its tail missing, and I was ashamed of it.

It didn't take me long to find the main road to Ismailia, and as soon as I was on it, I settled the Lagonda down to a steady sixty-five miles per hour. The road was narrow, but it had a smooth surface, and there was no traffic. The Delta country lay bleak and dismal around me in the

16

moonlight, the flat treeless fields, the ditches running between, and the black black soil everywhere. It was inexpressibly dreary.

But it didn't worry *me*. I was no part of it. I was completely isolated in my own luxurious little shell, as snug as a hermit crab and travelling a lot faster. Oh, how I do love to be on the move, winging away to new people and new places and leaving the old ones far behind! Nothing in the world exhilarates me more than that. And how I despise the average citizen, who settles himself down upon one tiny spot of land with one asinine woman, to breed and stew and rot in that condition unto his life's end. And always with the same woman! I cannot *believe* that any man in his senses would put up with just one female day after day and year after year. Some of them, of course, don't. But millions pretend they do.

I myself have never, absolutely never, permitted an intimate relationship to last for more than twelve hours. That is the farthest limit. Even eight hours is stretching it a bit, to my mind. Look what happened, for example, with Isabella. While we were upon the summit of the pyramid, she was a lady of scintillating parts, as pliant and playful as a puppy, and had I left her there to the mercy of those three Arab thugs, and skipped down on my own, all would have been well. But I foolishly stuck by her and helped her to descend, and as a result, the lovely lady turned into a vulgar screeching trollop, disgusting to behold.

What a world we live in! One gets no thanks these days for being chivalrous.

The Lagonda moved on smoothly through the night. Now for an opera. Which one should it be this time? I was in the mood for a Verdi. What about *Aida?* Of course! It must be *Aida* — the Egyptian opera! Most appropriate.

I began to sing. I was in exceptionally good voice tonight. I let myself go. It was delightful; and as I drove through the small town of Bilbeis, I was Aida herself, singing 'Numeipietà', the beautiful concluding passage of the first scene.

Half an hour later, at Zagazig, I was Amonasro begging the King of Egypt to save the Ethiopian captives with 'Ma tu, re, tu signore possente'.

Passing through El Abbasa, I was Rhadames, rendering 'Fuggiam gli adori nospiti', and now I opened all the windows of the car so that this incomparable love song might reach the ears of the fellaheen snoring in their hovels along the roadside, and perhaps mingle with their dreams.

As I pulled into Ismailia, it was six o'clock in the morning and the sun was already climbing high in a milky-blue heaven, but I myself was in the terrible sealed-up dungeon with Aida, singing 'O, terra, addio; addio valle di pianti!'

How swiftly the journey had gone. I drove to an hotel. The staff was just beginning to stir. I stirred them up some more and got the best room available. The sheets and blanket on the bed looked as though they had been slept in by twenty-five unwashed Egyptians on twenty-five consecutive nights, and I tore them off with my own hands (which I scrubbed immediately afterwards with antiseptic soap) and replaced them with my personal bedding. Then I set my alarm and slept soundly for two hours.

For breakfast I ordered a poached egg on a piece of toast. When the dish arrived — and I tell you, it makes my stomach curdle just to write about it — there was a *gleaming, curly, jet-black human hair*, three inches long, lying diagonally across the yolk of my poached egg. It was too much. I leaped up from the table and rushed out of the dining-room. '*Addio!*' I cried, flinging some money at the cashier as I went by, '*addio valle di pianti!*' And with that I shook the filthy dust of the hotel from my feet.

Now for the Sinai Desert. What a welcome change that would be. A real desert is one of the least contaminated places on earth, and Sinai was no exception. The road across it was a narrow strip of black tarmac about a hundred and forty miles long, with only a single filling station and a group of huts at the halfway mark, at a place called B'ir Rawd Salim. Otherwise there was nothing but pure uninhabited desert all the way. It would be very hot at this time of year, and it was essential to carry drinking water in case of a breakdown. I therefore pulled up outside a kind of general store in the main street of Ismailia to get my emergency canister refilled.

I went in and spoke to the proprietor. The man had a nasty case of trachoma. The granulation on the under surfaces of his eyelids was so acute that the lids themselves were raised right up off the eyeballs — a beastly sight. I asked him if he would sell me a gallon of *boiled* water. He thought I was mad, and madder still when I insisted on following him back into his

19

grimy kitchen to make sure that he did things properly. He filled a kettle with tap-water and placed it on a paraffin stove. The stove had a tiny little smoky yellow flame. The proprietor seemed very proud of the stove and of its performance. He stood admiring it, his head on one side. Then he suggested that I might prefer to go back and wait in the shop. He would bring me the water, he said, when it was ready. I refused to leave. I stood there watching the kettle like a lion, waiting for the water to boil; and while I was doing this, the breakfast scene suddenly started coming back to me in all its horror — the egg, the yolk, and the hair. Whose hair was it that had lain embedded in the slimy yolk of my egg at breakfast? Undoubtedly it was the cook's hair. And when, pray, had the cook last washed his head? He had probably never washed his head. Very well, then. He was almost certainly verminous. But that in itself would not cause a hair to fall out. What *did* cause the cook's hair, then, to fall out on to my poached egg this morning as he transferred the egg from the pan to the plate? There is a reason for all things, and in this case the reason was obvious. The cook's scalp was infested with purulent seborrhoeic impetigo. And the hair itself, the long black hair that I might so easily have swallowed had I been less alert, was therefore swarming with millions and millions of loving pathogenic cocci whose exact scientific name I have, happily, forgotten.

Can I, you ask, be absolutely sure that the cook had purulent seborrhoeic impetigo? Not absolutely sure — no. But if he hadn't, then he certainly had ringworm instead. And what did that mean? I knew only too well what it meant. It meant that ten million microsporons had been clinging and clustering around that awful hair, waiting to go into my mouth.

I began to feel sick.

'The water boils,' the shopkeeper said triumphantly.

'Let it boil,' I told him. 'Give it eight minutes more. What is it you want me to get — typhus?'

Personally, I never drink water by itself if I can help it, however pure it may be. Plain water has no flavour at all. I take it, of course, as tea or as coffee, but even then I try to arrange for bottled Vichy or Malvern to be used in the preparation. I avoid tap-water. Tap-water is diabolical stuff. Often it is nothing more nor less than reclaimed sewage.

'Soon this water will be boiled away in steam,' the proprietor said, grinning at me with green teeth.

I lifted the kettle myself and poured the contents into my canister.

Back in the shop, I bought six oranges, a small watermelon, and a slab of well-wrapped English chocolate. Then I returned to the Lagonda. Now at last I was away.

A few minutes later, I had crossed the sliding bridge that went over the Suez Canal just above Lake Timsah, and ahead of me lay the flat blazing desert and the little tarmac road stretching out before me like a black ribbon all the way to the horizon. I settled the Lagonda to the usual steady sixty-five miles an hour, and I

21

opened the windows wide. The air that came in was like the breath of an oven. The time was almost noon, and the sun was throwing its heat directly on to the roof of the car. My thermometer inside registered 103°. But as you know, a touch of warmth never bothers me so long as I am sitting still and am wearing suitable clothes — in this case a pair of cream-coloured linen slacks, a white aertex shirt, and a spider's-silk tie of the loveliest rich moss-green. I felt perfectly comfortable and at peace with the world.

For a minute or two I played with the idea of performing another opera *en route* — I was in the mood for *La Gioconda* — but after singing a few bars of the opening chorus, I began to perspire slightly; so I ran down the curtain, and lit a cigarette instead.

I was now driving through some of the finest scorpion country in the world, and I was eager to stop and make a search before I reached the halfway filling-station at B'ir Rawd Salim. I had so far met not a single vehicle or seen a living creature since leaving Ismailia an hour before. This pleased me. Sinai was authentic desert. I pulled up on the side of the road and switched off the engine. I was thirsty, so I ate an orange. Then I put my white topee on my head, and eased myself slowly out of the car, out of my comfortable hermit-crab shell, and into the sunlight. For a full minute I stood motionless in the middle of the road, blinking at the brilliance of the surroundings.

There was a blazing sun, a vast hot sky, and

beneath it all on every side a great pale sea of yellow sand that was not quite of this world. There were mountains now in the distance on the south side of the road, bare, pale-brown, tanagra-coloured mountains faintly glazed with blue and purple, that rose up suddenly out of the desert and faded away in a haze of heat against the sky. The stillness was overpowering. There was no sound at all, no voice of a bird or insect anywhere, and it gave me a queer godlike feeling to be standing there alone in the middle of such a splendid, hot, inhuman landscape — as though I were on another planet altogether, on Jupiter or Mars, or in some place more distant and desolate still, where never would the grass grow or the clouds turn red.

I went to the boot of the car and took out my killing-box, my net, and my trowel. Then I stepped off the road into the soft burning sand. I walked slowly for about a hundred yards into the desert, my eyes searching the ground. I was not looking for scorpions but the lairs of scorpions. The scorpion is a cryptozoic and nocturnal creature that hides all through the day either under a stone or in a burrow, according to its type. Only after the sun has gone down does it come out to hunt for food.

The one I wanted, opisthophthalmus, was a burrower, so I wasted no time turning over stones. I searched only for burrows. After ten or fifteen minutes, I had found none; but already the heat was getting to be too much for me, and I decided reluctantly to return to the car. I walked back very slowly, still watching the ground, and I had reached the road and was in the act of stepping on to it when all at once, in the sand, not more than twelve inches from the edge of the tarmac, I caught sight of a scorpion's burrow.

I put the killing-box and the net on the ground beside me. Then, with my little trowel, I began very cautiously to scrape away the sand all around the hole. This was an operation that never failed to excite me. It was like a treasure hunt — a treasure hunt with just the right amount of danger accompanying it to stir the blood. I could feel my heart beating away in my chest as I probed deeper and deeper into the sand.

And suddenly . . . there she was!

Oh, my heavens, what a whopper. A gigantic female scorpion, not opisthophthalmus, as I saw immediately, but pandinus, the other large African burrower. And clinging to her back — this was too good to be true! — swarming all over her, were one, two, three, four, five . . . a total of fourteen tiny babies! The mother was six inches long at least! Her children were the size of small revolver bullets. She had seen me now, the first human she had ever seen in her life, and her pincers were wide open, her tail was curled high over her back like a question mark, ready to strike. I took up the net, and slid it swiftly underneath her, and scooped her up. She twisted and squirmed, striking wildly in all directions with the end of her tail. I saw a single large drop of venom fall through the mesh into the sand. Quickly, I transferred her, together with the offspring, to the killing-box, and closed the lid. Then I fetched the ether from the car, and poured it through the little gauze hole in the top of the box until the pad inside was well soaked.

How splendid she would look in my collection! The babies would, of course, fall away from her as they died, but I would stick them on again with glue in more or less their correct positions; and then I would be the proud possessor of a huge female pandinus with her own fourteen offspring on her back! I was extremely pleased. I lifted the killing-box (I could feel her thrashing about furiously inside) and placed it in the boot, together with the net and trowel. Then I returned to my seat in the car, lit a cigarette, and drove on.

The more contented I am, the slower I drive. I drove quite slowly now, and it must have taken me nearly an hour more to reach B'ir Rawd Salim, the halfway station. It was a most unenticing place. On the left, there was a single gasoline pump and a wooden shack. On the right, there were three more shacks, each about the size of a potting-shed. The rest was desert. There was not a soul in sight. The time was twenty minutes before two in the afternoon, and the temperature inside the car was 106°.

What with the nonsense of getting the water boiled before leaving Ismailia, I had forgotten completely to fill up with gasoline before leaving, and my gauge was now registering slightly less than two gallons. I'd cut it rather fine — but no matter. I pulled in alongside the pump, and waited. Nobody appeared. I pressed the horn button, and the four tuned horns on the Lagonda shouted their wonderful *'Son gia mille e tre!'* across the desert. Nobody appeared. I pressed again.

sang the horns. Mozart's phrase sounded magnificent in these surroundings. But still nobody appeared. The inhabitants of B'ir Rawd Salim didn't give a damn, it seemed, about my friend Don Giovanni and the 1,003 women he had deflowered in Spain.

At last, after I had played the horns no less than six times, the door of the hut behind the gasoline pump opened and a tallish man emerged and stood on the threshold, doing up his buttons with both hands. He took his time over this, and not until he had finished did he glance up at the Lagonda. I looked back at him through my open window. I saw him take the first step in my direction . . . he took it very, very slowly . . . Then he took a second step . . .

My God! I thought at once. The spirochetes have got him!

He had the slow, wobbly walk, the loose-limbed, high-stepping gait of a man with locomotor ataxia. With each step he took, the front foot was raised high in the air before him and brought down violently to the ground, as though he were stamping on a dangerous insect.

I thought: I had better get out of here. I had

better start the motor and get the hell out of here before he reaches me. But I knew I couldn't. I *had* to have the gasoline. I sat in the car staring at the awful creature as he came stamping laboriously over the sand. He must have had the revolting disease for years and years, otherwise it wouldn't have developed into ataxis. *Tabes dorsalis* they call it in professional circles, and pathologically this means that the victim is suffering from degeneration of the posterior columns of the spinal chord. But ah my foes and oh my friends, it is really a lot worse than that; it is a slow and merciless consuming of the actual nerve fibres of the body by syphilitic toxins.

The man — the Arab, I shall call him — came right up to the door of my side of the car and peered in through the open window. I leaned away from him, praying that he would not come an inch closer. Without a doubt, he was one of the most blighted humans I had ever seen. His face had the eroded, eaten-away look of an old wood-carving when the worm has been at it, and the sight of it made me wonder how many other diseases the man was suffering from, besides syphilis.

'Salaam,' he mumbled.

'Fill up the tank,' I told him.

He didn't move. He was inspecting the interior of the Lagonda with great interest. A terrible feculent odour came wafting in from his direction.

'Come along!' I said sharply. 'I want some gasoline!'

He looked at me and grinned. It was more of a

leer than a grin, an insolent mocking leer that seemed to be saying, 'I am the king of the gasoline pump at B'ir Rawd Salim! Touch me if you dare!' A fly had settled in the corner of one of his eyes. He made no attempt to brush it away.

'You want gasoline?' he said, taunting me.

I was about to swear at him, but I checked myself just in time, and answered politely, 'Yes please, I would be very grateful.'

He watched me slyly for a few moments to be sure I wasn't mocking him, then he nodded as though satisfied now with my behaviour. He turned away and started slowly toward the rear of the car. I reached into the door-pocket for my bottle of Glenmorangie. I poured myself a stiff one, and sat sipping it. That man's face had been within a yard of my own; his foetid breath had come pouring into the car . . . and who knows how many billions of airborne viruses might not have come pouring in with it? On such an occasion it is a fine thing to sterilize the mouth and throat with a drop of Highland whisky. The whisky is also a solace. I emptied the glass, and poured myself another. Soon I began to feel less alarmed. I noticed the watermelon lying on the seat beside me. I decided that a slice of it at this moment would be refreshing. I took my knife from its case and cut out a thick section. Then, with the point of the knife, I carefully picked out all the black seeds, using the rest of the melon as a receptacle.

I sat drinking the whisky and eating the melon. Both very delicious.

'Gasoline is done,' the dreadful Arab said,

appearing at the window. 'I check water now, and oil.'

I would have preferred him to keep his hands off the Lagonda altogether, but rather than risk an argument, I said nothing. He went clumping off toward the front of the car, and his walk reminded me of a drunken Hitler Stormtrooper doing the goosestep in very slow motion.

Tabes dorsalis, as I live and breathe.

The only other disease to induce that queer high-stepping gait is chronic beriberi. Well — he probably had that one, too. I cut myself another slice of watermelon, and concentrated for a minute or so on taking out the seeds with the knife. When I looked up again, I saw that the Arab had raised the bonnet of the car on the righthand side, and was bending over the engine. His head and shoulders were out of sight, and so were his arms. What on earth was the man doing? The oil dipstick was on the other side. I rapped on the windshield. He seemed not to hear me. I put my head out of the window and shouted, 'Hey! Come out of there!'

Slowly, he straightened up, and as he drew his right arm out of the bowels of the engine, I saw that he was holding in his fingers something that was long and black and curly and very thin.

'Good God!' I thought. 'He's found a snake in there!'

He came round to the window, grinning at me and holding the object out for me to see; and only then, as I got a closer look, did I realize that it was not a snake at all — *it was the fan-belt of my Lagonda!*

All the awful implications of suddenly being stranded in this outlandish place with this disgusting man came flooding over me as I sat there staring dumbly at my broken fan-belt.

'You can see,' the Arab was saying, 'it was hanging on by a single thread. A good thing I noticed it.'

I took it from him and examined it closely. 'You cut it!' I cried.

'Cut it?' he answered softly. 'Why should I cut it?'

To be perfectly honest, it was impossible for me to judge whether he had or had not cut it. If he had, then he had also taken the trouble to fray the severed ends with some instrument to make it look like an ordinary break. Even so, my guess was that he *had* cut it, and if I was right then the implications were more sinister than ever.

'I suppose you know I can't go on without a fan-belt?' I said.

He grinned again with that awful mutilated mouth, showing ulcerated gums. 'If you go now,' he said, 'you will boil over in three minutes.'

'So what do you suggest?'

'I shall get you another fan-belt.'

'You will?'

'Of course. There is a telephone here, and if you will pay for the call, I will telephone to Ismailia. And if they haven't got one in Ismailia, I will telephone to Cairo. There is no problem.'

'No problem!' I shouted, getting out of the car. 'And when pray, do you think the fan-belt is going to arrive in this ghastly place?'

'There is a mail-truck comes through every

morning about ten o'clock. You would have it tomorrow.'

The man had all the answers. He never even had to think before replying.

This bastard, I thought, *has cut fan-belts before.*

I was very alert now, and watching him closely.

'They will not have a fan-belt for a machine of this make in Ismailia,' I said. 'It would have to come from the agents in Cairo. I will telephone them myself.' The fact that there was a telephone gave me some comfort. The telephone poles had followed the road all the way across the desert, and I could see the two wires leading into the hut from the nearest pole. 'I will ask the agents in Cairo to set out immediately for this place in a special vehicle,' I said.

The Arab looked along the road toward Cairo, some two hundred miles away. 'Who is going to drive six hours here and six hours back to bring a fan-belt?' he said. 'The mail will be just as quick.'

'Show me the telephone,' I said, starting toward the hut. Then a nasty thought struck me, and I stopped.

How could I possibly use this man's contaminated instrument? The earpiece would have to be pressed against my ear, and the mouthpiece would almost certainly touch my mouth; and I didn't give a damn what the doctors said about the impossibility of catching syphilis from remote contact. A syphilitic mouthpiece was a syphilitic mouthpiece, and you wouldn't catch *me* putting it anywhere near *my*

31

lips, thank you very much. I wouldn't even enter his hut.

I stood there in the sizzling heat of the afternoon and looked at the Arab with his ghastly diseased face, and the Arab looked back at me, as cool and unruffled as you please.

'You want the telephone?' he asked.

'No,' I said. 'Can you read English?'

'Oh, yes.'

'Very well. I shall write down for you the name of the agents and the name of this car, and also my own name. They know me there. You will tell them what is wanted. And listen . . . tell them to dispatch a special car immediately at my expense. I will pay them well. And if they won't do that, tell them they *have* to get the fan-belt to Ismailia in time to catch the mail-truck. You understand?'

'There is no problem,' the Arab said.

So I wrote down what was necessary on a piece of paper and gave it to him. He walked away with that slow, stamping tread toward the hut, and disappeared inside. I closed the bonnet of the car. Then I went back and sat in the driver's seat to think things out.

I poured myself another whisky, and lit a cigarette. There must be *some* traffic on this road. Somebody would surely come along before nightfall. But would that help me? No, it wouldn't — unless I were prepared to hitch a ride and leave the Lagonda and all my baggage behind to the tender mercies of the Arab. Was I prepared to do that? I didn't know. Probably yes. But if I were forced to stay the night, I would lock myself in the car and try to keep awake as much as possible. On no account would I enter the shack where that creature lived. Nor would I touch his food. I had whisky and water, and I had half a watermelon and a slab of chocolate. That was ample.

The heat was pretty bad. The thermometer in the car was still around 104°. It was hotter outside in the sun. I was perspiring freely. My God, what a place to get stranded in! And what a companion!

After about fifteen minutes, the Arab came out of the hut. I watched him all the way to the car.

'I talked to the garage in Cairo,' he said, pushing his face through the window. 'Fan-belt will arrive tomorrow by mail-truck. Everything arranged.'

'Did you ask them about sending it at once?'

'They said impossible,' he answered.

'You're sure you asked them?'

He inclined his head to one side and gave me that sly insolent grin. I turned away and waited for him to go. He stayed where he was. 'We have house for visitors,' he said. 'You can sleep there very nice. My wife will make food, but you will have to pay.'

'Who else is here besides you and your wife?'

'Another man,' he said. He waved an arm in the direction of the three shacks across the road, and I turned and saw a man standing in the doorway of the middle shack, a short wide man who was dressed in dirty khaki slacks and shirt. He was standing absolutely motionless in the shadow of the doorway, his arms dangling at his sides. He was looking at me.

'Who is he?' I said.

'Saleh.'

'What does he do?'

'He helps.'

'I will sleep in the car,' I said. 'And it will not be necessary for your wife to prepare food. I have my own.' The Arab shrugged and turned away and started back toward the shack where the telephone was. I stayed in the car. What else could I do? It was just after two-thirty. In three or four hours' time it would start to get a little cooler. Then I could take a stroll and maybe hunt up a few scorpions. Meanwhile, I must make the best of things as they were. I reached into the back of the car where I kept my box of books and, without looking, I took out the first one I touched. The box contained thirty or forty of the best books in the world, and all of them could be re-read a hundred times and would improve with each reading. It was immaterial which one I got. It turned out to be *The Natural History of Selborne*. I opened it at random . . .

' . . . We had in this village more than twenty years ago an idiot boy, whom I well remember, who, from a child, showed a strong propensity to bees; they were his food, his amusement, his sole object. And as people of this cast have seldom more than one point of view, so this lad exerted all his few faculties on this one pursuit. In winter he dozed away his time, within his father's house, by the fireside, in a kind of torpid state, seldom departing from the chimney-corner; but in the summer he was all alert, and in quest of

34

his game in the fields, and on sunny banks. Honey-bees, bumble-bees, wasps, were his prey wherever he found them; he had no apprehensions from their stings, but would seize them *nudis manibus*, and at once disarm them of their weapons, and suck their bodies for the sake of their honey-bags. Sometimes he would fill his bosom, between his shirt and his skin, with a number of these captives, and sometimes confine them to bottles. He was a very *merops apiaster*, or bee-bird, and very injurious to men that kept bees; for he would slide into their bee-gardens, and, sitting down before the stools, would rap with his fingers on the hives, and so take the bees as they came out. He has been known to overturn hives for the sake of honey, of which he is passionately fond. Where metheglin was making, he would linger round the tubs and vessels, begging a draught of what he called bee-wine. As he ran about, he used to make a humming noise with his lips, resembling the buzzing of bees . . . '

I glanced up from the book and looked around me. The motionless man across the road had disappeared. There was nobody in sight. The silence was eerie, and the stillness, the utter stillness and desolation of the place, was profoundly oppressive. I knew I was being watched. I knew that every little move I made, every sip of whisky and every puff of a cigarette, was being carefully noticed. I detest violence and I never carry a weapon. But I could have done with one now. For a while, I toyed with the idea of starting the motor and driving on down the road until the engine boiled over. But how far would I get? Not very far in this heat and without a fan. One mile, perhaps, or two at the most . . .

No — to hell with it. I would stay where I was and read my book.

It must have been about an hour later that I noticed a small dark speck moving toward me along the road in the far distance, coming from the Jerusalem direction. I laid aside my book without taking my eyes away from the speck. I watched it growing bigger and bigger. It was travelling at a great speed, at a really amazing speed. I got out of the Lagonda and hurried to the side of the road and stood there, ready to signal the driver to stop.

Closer and closer it came, and when it was about a quarter of a mile away, it began to slow down. Suddenly, I noticed the shape of its radiator. It was a *Rolls-Royce*! I raised an arm and kept it raised, and the big green car with a man at the wheel pulled in off the road and stopped beside my Lagonda.

I felt absurdly elated. Had it been a Ford or a Morris, I would have been pleased enough, but I would not have been elated. The fact that it was a Rolls — a Bentley would have done equally well, or an Isotta, or another Lagonda — was a virtual guarantee that I would receive all the assistance I required; for whether you know it or not, there is a powerful brotherhood existing among people who own very costly automobiles. They respect one another automatically, and the reason they respect one another is simply that wealth respects wealth. In point of fact, there is nobody in the world that a very wealthy person respects more than another very wealthy person, and because of this, they naturally seek each other out wherever they go. Recognition signals of many kinds are used among them. With the female, the wearing of massive jewels is perhaps the most common; but the costly automobile is also much favoured, and is used by both sexes. It is a travelling placard, a public declaration of affluence, and as such, it is also a card of membership to that excellent unofficial society, the Very-Wealthy-Peoples Union. I am a member myself of long standing, and am delighted to be one. When I meet another member, as I was about to do now, I feel an immediate rapport. I respect him. We speak the same language. He is one of *us*. I had good reason, therefore, to be elated.

The driver of the Rolls climbed out and came toward me. He was a small dark man with olive skin, and he wore an immaculate white linen suit. Probably a Syrian, I thought. Just possibly a Greek. In the heat of the day he looked as cool as could be.

'Good afternoon,' he said. 'Are you having trouble?'

I greeted him, and then bit by bit, I told him everything that had happened.

'My dear fellow,' he said in perfect English, 'but my *dear fellow*, how very distressing. What rotten luck. This is no place to get stranded in.'

'It isn't, is it?'

'And you say that a new fan-belt has definitely been ordered?'

'Yes,' I answered, 'if I can rely upon the proprietor of this establishment.'

The Arab, who had emerged from his shack almost before the Rolls had come to a stop, had now joined us, and the stranger proceeded to question him swiftly in Arabic about the steps he had taken on my behalf. It seemed to me that the two knew each other pretty well, and it was clear that the Arab was in great awe of the new arrival. He was practically crawling along the ground in his presence.

'Well — that seems to be all right,' the stranger said at last, turning to me. 'But quite obviously you won't be able to move on from here until tomorrow morning. Where were you headed for?'

'Jerusalem,' I said. 'And I don't relish the idea of spending the night in this infernal spot.'

'I should say not, my dear man. That would be most uncomfortable.' He smiled at me, showing exceptionally white teeth. Then he took out a cigarette case, and offered me a cigarette. The case was gold, and on the outside of it there was a thin line of green jade inlaid diagonally from corner to corner. It was a beautiful thing. I accepted the cigarette. He lit it for me, then lit his own.

The stranger took a long pull at his cigarette, inhaling deeply. Then he tilted back his head and blew the smoke up into the sun. 'We shall both get heat-stroke if we stand around here much longer,' he said. 'Will you permit me to make a suggestion?'

'But of course.'

'I do hope you won't consider it presumptuous, coming from a complete stranger . . . '

'Please . . . '

'You can't possibly remain here, so I suggest you come back and stay the night in my house.'

There! The Rolls-Royce was smiling at the Lagonda — smiling at it as it would never have smiled at a Ford or a Morris!

'You mean in Ismailia?' I said.

'No, no,' he answered, laughing. 'I live just around the corner, just over there.' He waved a hand in the direction he had come from.

'But surely you were going to Ismailia? I wouldn't want you to change your plans on my behalf.'

'I wasn't going to Ismailia at all,' he said. 'I was coming down here to collect the mail. My house — and this may surprise you — is quite close to where we are standing. You see that mountain. That's Maghara. I'm immediately behind it.'

I looked at the mountain. It lay about ten miles to the north, a yellow rocky lump, perhaps two thousand feet high. 'Do you really mean that you have a house in the middle of all this . . . this wasteland?' I asked.

'You don't believe me?' he said, smiling.

'Of course I believe you,' I answered. 'Nothing surprises me any more. Except, perhaps,' and here I smiled back at him, 'except when I meet a stranger in the middle of the desert, and he treats me like a brother. I am overwhelmed by your offer.'

'Nonsense, my dear fellow. My motives are entirely selfish. Civilized company is not easy to come by in these parts. I am quite thrilled at the thought of having a guest for dinner. Permit me to introduce myself — Abdul Aziz.' He made a quick little bow.

'Oswald Cornelius,' I said. 'It is a great pleasure.' We shook hands.

'I live partly in Beirut,' he said.

'I live in Paris.'

'Charming. And now — shall we go? Are you ready?'

'But my car,' I said. 'Can I leave it here safely?'

'Have no fear about that. Omar is a friend of mine. He's not much to look at, poor chap, but he won't let you down if you're with me. And the other one, Saleh, is a good mechanic. He'll fit your new fan-belt when it arrives tomorrow. I'll tell him now.'

Saleh, the man from across the road, had walked over while we were talking. Mr Aziz gave him his instructions. He then spoke to both men about guarding the Lagonda. He was brief and incisive. Omar and Saleh stood bowing and scraping. I went across to the Lagonda to get a suitcase. I needed a change of clothes badly.

'Oh, by the way,' Mr Aziz called over to me, 'I usually put on a black tie for dinner.'

'Of course,' I murmured, quickly pushing back my first choice of suitcase and taking another.

'I do it for the ladies mostly. They seem to like dressing themselves up for dinner.'

I turned sharply and looked at him, but he was already getting into his car.

'Ready?' he said.

I took the suitcase and placed it in the back of the Rolls. Then I climbed into the front seat

40

beside him, and we drove off.

During the drive, we talked casually about this and that. He told me that his business was in carpets. He had offices in Beirut and Damascus. His forefathers, he said, had been in the trade for hundreds of years.

I mentioned that I had a seventeenth-century Damascus carpet on the floor of my bedroom in Paris.

'You don't mean it!' he cried, nearly swerving off the road with excitement. 'Is it silk and wool, with the warp made entirely of silk? And has it got a ground of gold and silver threads?'

'Yes,' I said. 'Exactly.'

'But my dear fellow! You mustn't put a thing like that on the floor!'

'It is touched only by bare feet,' I said.

That pleased him. It seemed that he loved carpets almost as much as I loved the blue vases of Tchin-Hoa.

Soon we turned left off the tarred road on to a hard stony track and headed straight over the desert toward the mountain. 'This is my private driveway,' Mr Aziz said. 'It is five miles long.'

'You are even on the telephone,' I said, noticing the poles that branched off the main road to follow his private drive.

And then suddenly a queer thought struck me.

That Arab at the filling-station . . . he also was on the telephone . . .

Might not this, then, explain the fortuitous arrival of Mr Aziz?

Was it possible that my lonely host had devised a clever method of shanghai-ing travellers off the road in order to provide himself with what he called 'civilized company' for dinner? Had he, in fact, given the Arab standing instructions to immobilize the cars of all likely-looking persons one after the other as they came along? 'Just cut the fan-belt, Omar. Then phone me up quick. But make sure it's a decent-looking fellow with a good car. Then I'll pop along and see if I think he's worth inviting to the house . . . '

It was ridiculous of course.

'I think,' my companion was saying, 'that you are wondering why in the world I should choose to have a house out here in a place like this.'

'Well, yes, I am a bit.'

'Everyone does,' he said.

'*Everyone*,' I said.

'Yes,' he said.

Well, well, I thought — everyone.

'I live here,' he said, 'because I have a peculiar affinity with the desert. I am drawn to it the same way as a sailor is drawn to the sea. Does that seem so very strange to you?'

'No,' I answered, 'it doesn't seem strange at all.'

He paused and took a pull at his cigarette. Then he said, 'That is one reason. But there is another. Are you a family man, Mr Cornelius?'

'Unfortunately not,' I answered cautiously.

'I am,' he said. 'I have a wife and a daughter. Both of them, in my eyes at any rate, are very beautiful. My daughter is just eighteen. She has been to an excellent boarding-school in England, and she is now . . . ' he shrugged . . . 'she is now just sitting around and waiting until she is old enough to get married. But this waiting period — what does one do with a beautiful young girl during that time? I can't let her loose. She is far too desirable for that. When I take her to Beirut, I see the men hanging around her like wolves waiting to pounce. It drives me nearly out of my mind. I know all about men, Mr Cornelius. I know how they behave. It is true, of course, that I am not the only father who has had this problem. But the others seem somehow able to face it and accept it. They let their daughters go. They just turn them out of the house and look the other way. I cannot do that. I simply *cannot bring* myself to do it! I refuse to allow her to be mauled by every Achmed, Ali, and Hamil that comes along. And that, you see, is the other reason why I live in the desert — to protect my lovely child for a few more years from the wild beasts. Did you say that you had no family at all, Mr Cornelius?'

'I'm afraid that's true.'

'Oh.' He seemed disappointed. 'You mean you've never been married?'

'Well . . . no,' I said. 'No, I haven't.' I waited for the next inevitable question. It came about a minute later.

'Have you never *wanted* to get married and have children?'

They all asked that one. It was simply another way of saying, 'Are you, in that case, homosexual?'

'Once,' I said. 'Just once.'

'What happened?'

43

'There was only one person ever in my life, Mr Aziz . . . and after she went . . . ' I sighed.

'You mean she died?'

I nodded, too choked up to answer.

'My dear fellow,' he said. 'Oh, I am so sorry. Forgive me for intruding.'

We drove on for a while in silence.

'It's amazing,' I murmured, 'how one loses all interest in matters of the flesh after a thing like that. I suppose it's the shock. One never gets over it.'

He nodded sympathetically, swallowing it all.

'So now I just travel around trying to forget. I've been doing it for years . . . '

We had reached the foot of Mount Maghara now and were following the track as it curved around the mountain toward the side that was invisible from the road — the north side. 'As soon as we round the next bend you'll see the house,' Mr Aziz said.

We rounded the bend . . . and there it was! I blinked and stared, and I tell you that for the first few seconds I literally could not believe my eyes. I saw before me a white castle — I mean it — a *tall, white castle* with turrets and towers and little spires all over it, standing like a fairy-tale in the middle of a splash of green vegetation on the lower slope of the blazing-hot, bare, yellow mountain! It was fantastic! It was straight out of Hans Christian Andersen or Grimm. I had seen plenty of romantic-looking Rhine and Loire valley castles in my time, but never before had I seen anything with such a slender, graceful, fairy-tale quality as this! The greenery, as I observed when we drew closer, was a pretty garden of lawns and datepalms, and there was a high white wall going all the way round to keep out the desert.

'Do you approve?' my host asked, smiling.

'It's fabulous!' I said. 'It's like all the fairy-tale castles in the world made into one.'

'That's exactly what it is!' he cried. 'It's a fairy-tale castle! I built it especially for my daughter, my beautiful Princess.'

And the beautiful Princess is imprisoned within its walls by her strict and jealous father, King Abdul Aziz, who refuses to allow her the pleasures of masculine company. But watch out, for here comes Prince Oswald Cornelius to the rescue! Unbeknownst to the King, he is going to ravish the beautiful Princess, and make her very happy.

'You have to admit it's different,' Mr Aziz said.

'It is that.'

'It is also nice and private. I sleep very peacefully here. So does the Princess. No unpleasant young men are likely to come climbing in through *those* windows during the night.'

'Quite so,' I said.

'It used to be a small oasis,' he went on. 'I bought it from the government. We have ample water for the house, the swimming-pool, and three acres of garden.'

We drove through the main gates, and I must say it was wonderful to come suddenly into a miniature paradise of green lawns and flower-beds and palm-trees. Everything was in perfect order, and water-sprinklers were playing on the lawns. When we stopped at the front door of the house, two servants in spotless gallabiyahs and scarlet tarbooshes ran out immediately, one to each side of the car, to open the doors for us.

Two servants? But would both of them have come out like that unless they'd been expecting *two* people? I doubted it. More and more, it began to look as though my odd little theory about being shanghaied as a dinner guest was turning out to be correct. It was all very amusing.

My host ushered me in through the front door, and at once I got that lovely shivery feeling that comes over the skin as one walks suddenly out of intense heat into an air-conditioned room. I was standing in the hall. The floor was of green marble. On my right, there was a wide archway leading to a large room, and I received a fleeting impression of cool white walls, fine pictures, and superlative Louis XV furniture. What a place to find oneself in, in the middle of the Sinai Desert!

And now a woman was coming slowly down the stairs. My host had turned away to speak to the servants, and he didn't see her at once, so when she reached the bottom step, the woman paused, and she laid her naked arm like a white anaconda along the rail of the banister, and there she stood, looking at me as though she were Queen Semiramis on the steps of Babylon, and I was a candidate who might or might not be to her taste. Her hair was jet-black, and she had a figure that made me wet my lips.

When Mr Aziz turned and saw her, he said,

'Oh darling, there you are. I've brought you a guest. His car broke down at the filling-station — such rotten luck — so I asked him to come back and stay the night. Mr Cornelius . . . my wife.'

'How very nice,' she said quietly, coming forward.

I took her hand and raised it to my lips. 'I am overcome by your kindness, madame,' I murmured. There was, upon that hand of hers, a diabolical perfume. It was almost exclusively animal. The subtle, sexy secretions of the sperm-whale, the male musk-deer, and the beaver were all there, pungent and obscene beyond words; they dominated the blend completely, and only faint traces of the clean vegetable oils — lemon, cajuput, and zeroli — were allowed to come through. It was superb! And another thing I noticed in the flash of that first moment was this: When I took her hand, she did not, as other women do, let it lie limply across my palm like a fillet of raw fish. Instead, she placed her thumb *underneath* my hand, with the fingers on top; and thus she was able to — and I swear she did — exert a gentle but suggestive pressure upon my hand as I administered the conventional kiss.

'Where is Diana?' asked Mr Aziz.

'She's out by the pool,' the woman said. And turning to me, 'Would *you* like a swim, Mr Cornelius? You must be roasted after hanging around that awful filling-station.'

She had huge velvet eyes, so dark they were almost black, and when she smiled at me, the end of her nose moved upwards, distending the nostrils.

There and then, Prince Oswald Cornelius decided that he cared not one whit about the beautiful Princess who was held captive in the castle by the jealous King. He would ravish the Queen instead.

'Well . . . ' I said.

'I'm going to have one,' Mr Aziz said.

'Let's all have one,' his wife said. 'We'll lend you a pair of trunks.'

I asked if I might go up to my room first and get out a clean shirt and clean slacks to put on after the swim, and my hostess said, 'Yes, of course,' and told one of the servants to show me the way. He took me up two flights of stairs, and we entered a large white bedroom which had in it an exceptionally large double-bed. There was a well-equipped bathroom leading off to one side, with a pale-blue bathtub and a bidet to match. Everywhere, things were scrupulously clean and very much to my liking. While the servant was unpacking my case, I went over to the window and looked out, and I saw the great blazing desert sweeping in like a yellow sea all the way from the horizon until it met the white garden wall just below me, and there, within the wall, I could see the swimming-pool, and beside the pool there was a girl lying on her back in the shade of a big pink parasol. The girl was wearing a white swimming costume, and she was reading a book. She had long slim legs and black hair. She was the Princess.

What a set-up, I thought. The white castle, the

comfort, the cleanliness, the air-conditioning, the two dazzlingly beautiful females, the watchdog husband, and a whole evening to work in! The situation was so perfectly designed for my entertainment that it would have been impossible to improve upon it. The problems that lay ahead appealed to me very much. A simple straightforward seduction did not amuse me any more. There was no artistry in that sort of thing; and I can assure you that had I been able, by waving a magic wand, to make Mr Abdul Aziz, the jealous watchdog, disappear for the night, I would not have done so. I wanted no pyrrhic victories.

When I left the room, the servant accompanied me. We descended the first flight of stairs, and then, on the landing of the floor below my own, I paused and said casually, 'Does the whole family sleep on this floor?'

'Oh, yes,' the servant said. 'That is the master's room there' — indicating a door — 'and next to it is Mrs Aziz. Miss Diana is opposite.'

Three separate rooms. All very close together. Virtually impregnable. I tucked the information away in my mind and went on down to the pool. My host and hostess were there before me.

'This is my daughter, Diana,' my host said.

The girl in the white swimming-suit stood up and I kissed her hand. 'Hello, Mr Cornelius,' she said.

She was using the same heavy animal perfume as her mother — ambergris, musk, and castor! What a smell it had — bitchy, brazen, and marvellous! I sniffed at it like a dog. She was, I

49

thought, even more beautiful than the parent, if that were possible. She had the same large velvety eyes, the same black hair, and the same shape of face; but her legs were unquestionably longer, and there was something about her body that gave it a slight edge over the older woman's: it was more sinuous, more snaky, and almost certain to be a good deal more flexible. But the older woman, who was probably thirty-seven and looked no more than twenty-five, had a spark in her eye that the daughter could not possibly match.

Eeeny, meeny, miny, mo — just a little while ago, Prince Oswald had sworn that he would ravish the Queen alone, and to hell with the Princess. But now that he had seen the Princess in the flesh, he did not know which one to prefer. Both of them, in their different ways, held forth a promise of innumerable delights, the one innocent and eager, the other expert and voracious. The truth of the matter was that he would like to have them both — the Princess as an hors d'oeuvre, and the Queen as the main dish.

'Help yourself to a pair of trunks in the changing-room, Mr Cornelius,' Mrs Aziz was saying, so I went into the hut and changed, and when I came out again the three of them were already splashing about in the water. I dived in and joined them. The water was so cold it made me gasp.

'I thought that would surprise you,' Mr Aziz said, laughing. 'It's cooled. I keep it at sixty-five degrees. It's more refreshing in this climate.'

Later, when the sun began dropping lower in the sky, we all sat around in our wet swimming-clothes while a servant brought us pale, ice-cold martinis, and it was at this point that I began, very slowly, very cautiously, to seduce the two ladies in my own particular fashion. Normally, when I am given a free hand, this is not especially difficult for me to do. The curious little talent that I happen to possess — the ability to hypnotize a woman with words — very seldom lets me down. It is not, of course, done only with words. The words themselves, the innocuous, superficial words, are spoken only by the mouth, whereas the real message, the improper and exciting promise, comes from all the limbs and organs of the body, and is transmitted through the eyes. More than that I cannot honestly tell you about how it is done. The point is that it works. It works like cantharides. I believe that I could sit down opposite the Pope's wife, if he had one, and within fifteen minutes, were I to try hard enough, she would be leaning toward me over the table with her lips apart and her eyes glazed with desire. It is a minor talent, not a great one, but I am nonetheless thankful to have had it bestowed upon me, and I have done my best at all times to see that it has not been wasted.

So the four of us, the two wondrous women, the little man, and myself, sat close together in a semi-circle beside the swimming-pool, lounging in deck-chairs and sipping our drinks and feeling the warm six o'clock sunshine upon our skin. I was in good form. I made them laugh a great deal. The story about the greedy old Duchess of Glasgow putting her hand in the chocolate-box and getting nipped by one of my scorpions had the daughter falling out of her chair with mirth; and when I described in detail the interior of my spider breeding-house in the garden outside Paris, both ladies began wriggling with revulsion and pleasure.

It was at this stage that I noticed the eyes of Mr Abdul Aziz resting upon me in a good-humoured, twinkling kind of way. 'Well, well,' the eyes seemed to be saying, 'we are glad to see that you are not quite so disinterested in women as you led us to believe in the car . . . Or is it, perhaps, that these congenial surroundings are helping you to forget that great sorrow of yours at last . . . ' Mr Aziz smiled at me, showing his pure white teeth. It was a friendly smile. I gave him a friendly smile back. What a friendly little fellow he was. He was genuinely delighted to see me paying so much attention to the ladies. So far, then, so good.

I shall skip very quickly over the next few hours, for it was not until after midnight that anything really tremendous happened to me. A few brief notes will suffice to cover the intervening period:

At seven o'clock, we all left the swimming-pool and returned to the house to dress for dinner.

At eight o'clock, we assembled in the big living-room to drink another cocktail. The two ladies were both superbly turned out, and sparkling with jewels. Both of them wore lowcut, sleeveless evening-dresses which had come, without any doubt at all, from some great fashion house in Paris. My hostess was in black, her daughter in pale blue, and the scent of that intoxicating perfume was everywhere about them. What a pair they were! The older woman had that slight forward hunch to her shoulders which one sees only in the most passionate and practised of females; for in the same way as a horsey woman will become bandy-legged from sitting constantly upon a horse, so a woman of great passion will develop a curious roundness of the shoulders from continually embracing men. It is an occupational deformity, and the noblest of them all.

The daughter was not yet old enough to have acquired this singular badge of honour, but with her it was enough for me simply to stand back and observe the shape of her body and to notice the splendid sliding motion of her thighs underneath the tight silk dress as she wandered about the room. She had a line of tiny soft golden hairs growing all the way up the exposed length of her spine, and when I stood behind her it was difficult to resist the temptation of running my knuckles up and down those lovely vertebrae.

At eight thirty, we moved into the dining-room. The dinner that followed was a really magnificent affair, but I shall waste no time here describing food or wine. Throughout the meal I continued to play most delicately and insidiously upon the sensibilities of the women, employing every skill that I possessed; and by the time the dessert arrived, they were melting before my eyes

53

like butter in the sun.

After dinner we returned to the living-room for coffee and brandy, and then, at my host's suggestion, we played a couple of rubbers of bridge.

By the end of the evening, I knew for certain that I had done my work well. The old magic had not let me down. Either of the two ladies, should circumstances permit, was mine for the asking. I was not deluding myself over this. It was a straightforward, obvious fact. It stood out a mile. The face of my hostess was bright with excitement, and whenever she looked at me across the card-table, those huge dark velvety eyes would grow bigger and bigger, and the nostrils would dilate, and the mouth would open slightly to reveal the tip of a moist pink tongue squeezing through between the teeth. It was a marvellously lascivious gesture, and more than once it caused me to trump my own trick. The daughter was less daring but equally direct. Each time her eyes met mine, and that was often enough, she would raise her brows just the tiniest fraction of a centimetre, as though asking a question; then she would make a quick sly little smile, supplying the answer.

'I think it's time we all went to bed,' Mr Aziz said, examining his watch. 'It's after eleven. Come along, my dears.'

Then a queer thing happened. At once, without a second's hesitation and without another glance in my direction, both ladies rose and made for the door! It was astonishing. It left me stunned. I didn't know what to make of it. It was the quickest thing I'd ever seen. And yet it wasn't as though Mr Aziz had spoken angrily. His voice, to me at any rate, had sounded as pleasant as ever. But now he was already turning out the lights, indicating clearly that he wished me also to retire. What a blow! I had expected at least to receive a whisper from either the wife or the daughter before we separated for the night, just a quick three or four words telling me where to go and when; but instead, I was left standing like a fool beside the card-table while the two ladies glided out of the room.

My host and I followed them up the stairs. On the landing of the first floor, the mother and daughter stood side by side, waiting for me.

'Good night, Mr Cornelius,' my hostess said.

'Good night, Mr Cornelius,' the daughter said.

'Good night, my dear fellow,' Mr Aziz said. 'I do hope you have everything you want.'

They turned away, and there was nothing for me to do but continue slowly, reluctantly, up the second flight of stairs to my own room. I entered it and closed the door. The heavy brocade curtains had already been drawn by one of the servants but I parted them and leaned out the window to take a look at the night. The air was still and warm, and a brilliant moon was shining over the desert. Below me, the swimming-pool in the moonlight looked something like an enormous glass mirror lying flat on the lawn, and beside it I could see the four deck-chairs we had been sitting in earlier.

Well, well, I thought. What happens now?

One thing I knew I must not do in this house

was to venture out of my room and go prowling around the corridors. That would be suicide. I had learned many years ago that there are three breeds of husband with whom one must never take unnecessary risks — the Bulgarian, the Greek, and the Syrian. None of them, for some reason, resents you flirting quite openly with his wife, but he will kill you at once if he catches you getting into her bed. Mr Aziz was a Syrian. A degree of prudence was therefore essential, and if any move were going to be made now, it must be made not by me but by one of the two women, for only she (or they) would know precisely what was safe and what was dangerous. Yet I had to admit that after witnessing the way in which my host had called them both to heel four minutes ago, there was little hope of further action in the near future. The trouble was, though, that I had got myself so infernally steamed up.

I undressed and took a long cold shower. That helped. Then, because I have never been able to sleep in the moonlight, I made sure that the curtains were tightly drawn together. I got into bed, and for the next hour or so I lay reading some more of Gilbert White's *Natural History of Selborne*. That also helped, and at last, somewhere between midnight and one a.m., there came a time when I was able to switch out the light and prepare myself for sleep without altogether too many regrets.

I was just beginning to doze off when I heard some tiny sounds. I recognized them at once. They were sounds that I had heard many times before in my life, and yet they were still, for me, the most thrilling and evocative in the whole world. They consisted of a series of little soft metallic noises, of metal grating gently against metal, and they were made, they were always made by somebody who was very slowly, very cautiously, turning the handle of one's door from the outside. Instantly, I became wide awake. But I did not move. I simply opened my eyes and stared in the direction of the door; and I can remember wishing at that moment for a gap in the curtain, for just a small thin shaft of moonlight to come in from outside so that I could at least catch a glimpse of the shadow of the lovely form that was about to enter. But the room was as dark as a dungeon.

I did not hear the door open. No hinge squeaked. But suddenly a little gust of air swept through the room and rustled the curtains, and a moment later I heard the soft thud of wood against wood as the door was carefully closed again. Then came the click of the latch as the handle was released.

Next, I heard feet tiptoeing toward me over the carpet.

For one horrible second, it occurred to me that this might just possibly be Mr Abdul Aziz creeping in upon me with a long knife in his hand, but then all at once a warm extensile body was bending over mine, and a woman's voice was whispering in my ear, '*Don't make a sound!*'

'My dearest beloved,' I said, wondering which one of them it was, 'I knew you'd . . . ' Instantly her hand came over my mouth.

'*Please!*' she whispered. '*Not another word!*'

I didn't argue. My lips had many better things to do than that. So had hers.

Here I must pause. This is not like me at all — I know that. But just for once, I wish to be excused a detailed description of the great scene that followed. I have my own reasons for this and I beg you to respect them. In any case, it will do you no harm to exercise your own imagination for a change, and if you wish, I will stimulate it a little by saying simply and truthfully that of the many thousands and thousands of women I have known in my time, none has transported me to greater extremes of ecstasy than this lady of the Sinai Desert. Her dexterity was amazing. Her passion was intense. Her range was unbelievable. At every turn, she was ready with some new and intricate manoeuvre. And to cap it all, she possessed the subtlest and most recondite style I have ever encountered. She was a great artist. She was a genius.

All this, you will probably say, indicated clearly that my visitor must have been the older woman. You would be wrong. It indicated nothing. True genius is a gift of birth. It has very little to do with age; and I can assure you I had no way of knowing for certain which of them it was in the darkness of that room. I wouldn't have bet a penny on it either way. At one moment, after some particularly boisterous cadenza, I would be convinced it was the wife. *It must be the wife!* Then suddenly the whole tempo would begin to change, and the melody would become so childlike and innocent that I found myself swearing it was the daughter. *It must be the daughter!*

Maddening it was not to know the true answer. It tantalized me. It also humbled me, for, after all, a connoisseur, a supreme connoisseur, should always be able to guess the vintage without seeing the label on the bottle. But this one really had me beat. At one point, I reached for cigarettes, intending to solve the mystery in the flare of a match, but her hand was on me in a flash, and cigarettes and matches were snatched away and flung across the room. More than once, I began to whisper the question itself into her ear, but I never got three words out before the hand shot up again and smacked itself over my mouth. Rather violently, too.

Very well, I thought. Let it be for now. Tomorrow morning, downstairs in the daylight, I shall know for certain which one of you it was. I shall know by the glow on the face, by the way the eyes look back into mine, and by a hundred other little telltale signs. I shall also know by the marks that my teeth have made on the left side of the neck, above the dress line. A rather wily move, that one, I thought, and so perfectly timed — my vicious bite was administered during the height of her passion — that she never for one moment realized the significance of the act.

It was altogether a most memorable night, and at least four hours must have gone by before she gave me a final fierce embrace, and slipped out of the room as quickly as she had come in.

The next morning I did not awaken until after ten o'clock. I got out of bed and drew open the curtains. It was another brilliant, hot, desert day. I took a leisurely bath, then dressed myself as carefully as ever. I felt relaxed and chipper. It made me very happy to think that I could still summon a woman to my room with my eyes alone, even in middle age. And what a woman! It would be fascinating to find out which one of them she was. I would soon know.

I made my way slowly down the two flights of stairs.

'Good morning, my dear fellow, good morning!' Mr Aziz said, rising from a small desk he had been writing at in the living-room. 'Did you have a good night?'

'Excellent, thank you,' I answered, trying not to sound smug.

He came and stood close to me, smiling with his very white teeth. His shrewd little eyes rested on my face and moved over it slowly, as though searching for something.

'I have good news for you,' he said. 'They called up from B'ir Rawd Salim five minutes ago and said your fan-belt had arrived by the mail-truck. Saleh is fitting it on now. It'll be ready in an hour. So when you've had some breakfast, I'll drive you over and you can be on your way.'

I told him how grateful I was.

'We'll be sorry to see you go,' he said. 'It's been an immense pleasure for all of us having you drop in like this, an immense pleasure.'

I had my breakfast alone in the dining-room. Afterwards, I returned to the living-room to smoke a cigarette while my host continued writing at his desk.

'Do forgive me,' he said. 'I just have a couple of things to finish here. I won't be long. I've arranged for your case to be packed and put in the car, so you have nothing to worry about. Sit down and enjoy your cigarette. The ladies ought to be down any minute now.'

The wife arrived first. She came sailing into the room looking more than ever like the dazzling Queen Semiramis of the Nile, and the first thing I noticed about her was the pale-green chiffon scarf knotted casually around her neck! Casually but carefully! So carefully that no part of the skin of the neck was visible. The woman went straight over to her husband and kissed him on the cheek. 'Good morning, my darling,' she said.

You cunning beautiful bitch, I thought.

'Good *morning*, Mr Cornelius,' she said gaily, coming over to sit in the chair opposite mine. 'Did you have a good night? I do hope you had everything you wanted.'

Never in my life have I seen such a sparkle in a woman's eyes as I saw in hers that morning, nor such a glow of pleasure in a woman's face.

'I had a very good night indeed, thank *you*,' I answered, showing her that I knew.

She smiled and lit a cigarette. I glanced over at Mr Aziz, who was still writing away busily at the desk with his back to us. He wasn't paying the slightest attention to his wife or to me. He was, I thought, exactly like all the other poor cuckolds that I ever created. Not one of them would believe that it could happen to him, not right under his own nose.

'Good morning, everybody!' cried the daughter, sweeping into the room. 'Good morning, daddy! Good morning, mummy!' She gave them each a kiss. 'Good morning, Mr Cornelius!' She was wearing a pair of pink slacks and a rust-coloured blouse, and I'll be damned if she didn't also have a scarf tied carelessly but carefully around her neck! A chiffon scarf!

'Did you have a decent night?' she asked, perching herself like a young bride on the arm of my chair, arranging herself in such a way that one of her thighs rested against my forearm. I leaned back and looked at her closely. She looked back at me and winked. She actually winked! Her face was glowing and sparkling every bit as much as her mother's, and if anything, she seemed even more pleased with herself than the older woman.

I felt pretty confused. Only one of them had a bite mark to conceal, yet both of them had covered their necks with scarves. I conceded that this might be a coincidence, but on the face of it, it looked much more like a conspiracy to me. It looked as though they were both working closely together to keep me from discovering the truth. But what an extraordinary screwy business! And what was the purpose of it all? And in what other peculiar ways, might I ask, did they plot and plan together among themselves? Had they drawn lots or something the night before? Or did they simply take it in turns with visitors? I *must* come back again, I told myself, for another visit as soon as possible just to see what happens the next time. In fact, I might motor down specially from Jerusalem in a day or two. It would be easy, I reckoned, to get myself invited again.

'Are you ready, Mr Cornelius?' Mr Aziz said, rising from his desk.

'Quite ready,' I answered.

The ladies, sleek and smiling, led the way outside to where the big green Rolls-Royce was waiting. I kissed their hands and murmured a million thanks to each of them. Then I got into the front seat beside my host, and we drove off. The mother and daughter waved. I lowered my window and waved back. Then we were out of the garden and into the desert, following the stony yellow track as it skirted the base of Mount Maghara, with the telegraph poles marching along beside us.

During the journey, my host and I conversed pleasantly about this and that. I was at pains to be as agreeable as possible because my one object now was to get myself invited to stay at the house again. If I didn't succeed in getting *him* to ask *me*, then *I* should have to ask *him*. I would do it at the last moment. 'Good-bye, my dear friend,' I would say, gripping him warmly by the throat. 'May I have the pleasure of dropping in to see you again if I happen to be passing this way?' And of course he would say yes.

'Did you think I exaggerated when I told you my daughter was beautiful?' he asked me.

'You understated it,' I said. 'She's a raving beauty. I do congratulate you. But your wife is no less lovely. In fact, between the two of them they almost swept me off my feet,' I added, laughing.

'I noticed that,' he said, laughing with me. 'They're a couple of very naughty girls. They do so love to flirt with other men. But why should I mind. There's no harm in flirting.'

'None whatsoever,' I said.

'I think it's gay and fun.'

'It's charming,' I said.

In less than half an hour we had reached the main Ismailia — Jerusalem road. Mr Aziz turned the Rolls on to the black tarmac strip and headed for the filling-station at seventy miles an hour. In a few minutes we would be there. So now I tried moving a little closer to the subject of another visit, fishing gently for an invitation. 'I can't get over your house,' I said. 'I think it's simply wonderful.'

'It is nice, isn't it?'

'I suppose you're bound to get pretty lonely out there, on and off, just the three of you together?'

'It's no worse than anywhere else,' he said. 'People get lonely wherever they are. A desert, or a city — it doesn't make much difference, really. But we do have visitors, you know. You'd be surprised at the number of people who drop in from time to time. Like you, for instance. It was a great pleasure having you with us, my dear fellow.'

'I shall never forget it,' I said. 'It is a rare thing to find kindness and hospitality of that order nowadays.'

I waited for him to tell me that I must come again, but he didn't. A little silence sprang up between us, a slightly uneasy little silence. To bridge it, I said, 'I think yours is the most thoughtful paternal gesture I've ever heard of in my life.'

'Mine?'

'Yes. Building a house right out there in the back of beyond and living in it just for your daughter's sake, to protect her. I think it's remarkable.'

I saw him smile, but he kept his eyes on the road and said nothing. The filling-station and the group of huts were now in sight about a mile ahead of us. The sun was high and it was getting hot inside the car.

'Not many fathers would put themselves out to that extent,' I went on.

Again he smiled, but somewhat bashfully, this time, I thought. And then he said, 'I don't deserve *quite* as much credit as you like to give me, really I don't. To be absolutely honest with you, that pretty daughter of mine isn't the only reason for my living in such splendid isolation.'

'I know that.'

'You do?'

'You told me. You said the other reason was the desert. You loved it, you said, as a sailor loves the sea.'

'So I did. And it's quite true. But there's still a third reason.'

'Oh, and what is that?'

He didn't answer me. He sat quite still with his hands on the wheel and his eyes fixed on the road ahead.

'I'm sorry,' I said. 'I shouldn't have asked the question. It's none of my business.'

65

'No, no, that's quite all right,' he said. 'Don't apologize.'

I stared out of the window at the desert. 'I think it's hotter than yesterday,' I said. 'It must be well over a hundred already.'

'Yes.'

I saw him shifting a little in his seat, as though trying to get comfortable, and then he said, 'I don't really see why I shouldn't tell you the truth about that house. You don't strike me as being a gossip.'

'Certainly not,' I said.

We were close to the filling-station now, and he had slowed the car down almost to walking-speed to give himself time to say what he had to say. I could see the two Arabs standing beside my Lagonda, watching us.

'That daughter,' he said at length, 'the one you met she isn't the only daughter I have.'

'Oh, really?'

'I've got another who is five years older than she.'

'And just as beautiful, no doubt,' I said. 'Where does she live? In Beirut?'

'No, she's in the house.'

'In which house? Not the one we've just left?'

'Yes.'

'But I never saw her!'

'Well,' he said, turning suddenly to watch my face, 'maybe not.'

'But why?'

'She had leprosy.'

I jumped.

'Yes, I know,' he said, 'it's a terrible thing. She

66

has the worst kind, too, poor girl. It's called anaesthetic leprosy. It is highly resistant, and almost impossible to cure. If only it were the nodular variety, it would be much easier. But it isn't, and there you are. So when a visitor comes to the house, she keeps to her own apartment, on the third floor . . . '

The car must have pulled into the filling-station about then because the next thing I can remember was seeing Mr Abdul Aziz sitting there looking at me with those small clever black eyes of his, and he was saying, 'But my dear fellow, you mustn't alarm yourself like this. Calm yourself down, Mr Cornelius, calm yourself down! There's absolutely nothing in the world for you to worry about. It is not a very contagious disease. You have to have the most *intimate* contact with the person in order to catch it . . . '

I got out of the car very slowly and stood in the sunshine. The Arab with the diseased face was grinning at me and saying, 'Fan-belt all fixed now. Everything fine.' I reached into my pocket for cigarettes, but my hand was shaking so violently I dropped the packet on the ground. I bent down and retrieved it. Then I got a cigarette out and managed to light it. When I looked up again, I saw the green Rolls-Royce already half a mile down the road, and going away fast.

The Great Switcheroo

There were about forty people at Jerry and Samantha's cocktail-party that evening. It was the usual crowd, the usual discomfort, the usual appalling noise. People had to stand very close to one another and shout to make themselves heard. Many were grinning, showing capped white teeth. Most of them had a cigarette in the left hand, a drink in the right.

I moved away from my wife Mary and her group. I headed for the small bar in the far corner, and when I got there, I sat down on a bar-stool and faced the room. I did this so that I could look at the women. I settled back with my shoulders against the bar-rail, sipping my Scotch and examining the women one by one over the rim of my glass.

I was studying not their figures but their faces, and what interested me there was not so much the face itself but the big red mouth in the middle of it all. And even then, it wasn't the whole mouth but only the lower lip. The lower lip, I had recently decided, was the great revealer. It gave away more than the eyes. The eyes hid their secrets. The lower lip hid very little. Take, for example, the lower lip of Jacinth Winkleman, who was standing nearest to me. Notice the wrinkles on that lip, how some were parallel and some radiated outward. No two people had the same pattern of lip-wrinkles, and come to think of it, you could catch a criminal that way if you had his lip-print on file and he had taken a drink at the scene of the crime. The lower lip is what you suck and nibble when you're ruffled, and Martha Sullivan was doing that right now as she watched from a distance her fatuous husband slobbering over Judy Martinson. You lick it when lecherous. I could see Ginny Lomax licking hers with the tip of her tongue as she stood beside Ted Dorling and gazed up into his face. It was a deliberate lick, the tongue coming out slowly and making a slow wet wipe along the entire length of the lower lip. I saw Ted Dorling looking at Ginny's tongue, which was what she wanted him to do.

It really does seem to be a fact, I told myself, as my eyes wandered from lower lip to lower lip across the room, that all the less attractive traits of the human animal, arrogance, rapacity, gluttony, lasciviousness, and the rest of them, are clearly signalled in that little carapace of scarlet skin. But you have to know the code. The protuberant or bulging lower lip is supposed to signify sensuality. But this is only half true in men and wholly untrue in women. In women, it is the thin line you should look for, the narrow blade with the sharply delineated bottom edge. And in the nymphomaniac there is a tiny just visible crest of skin at the top centre of the lower lip.

Samantha, my hostess, had that.

Where was she now, Samantha?

Ah, there she was, taking an empty glass out of a guest's hand. Now she was heading my way to refill it.

'Hello, Vic,' she said. 'You all alone?'

She's a nympho-bird all right, I told myself. But a very rare example of the species, because she is entirely and utterly monogamous. She is a married monogamous nympho-bird who stays for ever in her own nest.

She is also the fruitiest female I have ever set eyes upon in my whole life.

'Let me help you,' I said, standing up and taking the glass from her hand. 'What's wanted in here?'

'Vodka on the rocks,' she said. 'Thanks, Vic.' She laid a lovely long white arm upon the top of the bar and she leaned forward so that her bosom rested on the bar-rail, squashing upward. 'Oops,' I said, pouring vodka outside the glass.

Samantha looked at me with huge brown eyes, but said nothing.

'I'll wipe it up,' I said.

She took the refilled glass from me and walked away. I watched her go. She was wearing black pants. They were so tight around the buttocks that the smallest mole or pimple would have shown through the cloth. But Samantha Rainbow had not a blemish on her bottom. I caught myself licking my own lower lip. That's right, I thought. I want her. I lust after that woman. But it's too risky to try. It would be suicide to make a pass at a girl like that. First of all, she lives next door, which is too close. Secondly, as I have already said, she is monogamous. Thirdly, she is thick as a thief with Mary, my own wife. They exchange dark female secrets. Fourthly, her husband Jerry is my very

70

old and good friend, and not even I, Victor Hammond, though I am churning with lust, would dream of trying to seduce the wife of a man who is my very old and trusty friend.

Unless . . .

It was at this point, as I sat on the bar-stool letching over Samantha Rainbow, that an interesting idea began to filter quietly into the centre of my brain. I remained still, allowing the idea to expand. I watched Samantha across the room, and began fitting her into the framework of the idea. Oh, Samantha, my gorgeous and juicy little jewel, I shall have you yet.

But could anybody seriously hope to get away with a crazy lark like that?

No, not in a million nights.

One couldn't even *try* it unless Jerry agreed. So why think about it?

Samantha was standing about six yards away, talking to Gilbert Mackesy. The fingers of her right hand were curled around a tall glass. The fingers were long and almost certainly dexterous.

Assuming, just for the fun of it, that Jerry did agree, then even so, there would still be gigantic snags along the way. There was, for example, the little matter of physical characteristics. I had seen Jerry many times at the club having a shower after tennis, but right now I couldn't for the life of me recall the necessary details. It wasn't the sort of thing one noticed very much. Usually, one didn't even look.

Anyway, it would be madness to put the suggestion to Jerry point-blank. I didn't know him *that* well. He might be horrified. He might even turn nasty. There could be an ugly scene. I must test him out, therefore, in some subtle fashion.

'You know something,' I said to Jerry about an hour later when we were sitting together on the sofa having a last drink. The guests were drifting away and Samantha was by the door saying goodbye to them. My own wife Mary was out on the terrace talking to Bob Swain. I could see through the open French windows. 'You know something funny?' I said to Jerry as we sat together on the sofa.

'What's funny?' Jerry asked me.

'A fellow I had lunch with today told me a fantastic story. Quite unbelievable.'

'What story?' Jerry said. The whisky had begun to make him sleepy.

'This man, the one I had lunch with, had a terrific letch after the wife of his friend who lived nearby. And his friend had an equally big letch after the wife of the man I had lunch with. Do you see what I mean?'

'You mean two fellers who lived close to each other both fancied each other's wives.'

'Precisely,' I said.

'Then there was no problem,' Jerry said.

'There was a very big problem,' I said. 'The wives were both very faithful and honourable women.'

'Samantha's the same,' Jerry said. 'She wouldn't look at another man.'

'Nor would Mary,' I said. 'She's a fine girl.'

Jerry emptied his glass and set it down carefully on the sofa-table. 'So what happened in your story?' he said. 'It sounds dirty.'

'What happened,' I said, 'was that these two randy sods cooked up a plan which made it possible for each of them to ravish the other's wife without the wives ever knowing it. If you can believe such a thing.'

'With chloroform?' Jerry said.

'Not at all. They were fully conscious.'

'Impossible,' Jerry said. 'Someone's been pulling your leg.'

'I don't think so,' I said. 'From the way this man told it to me, with all the little details and everything, I don't think he was making it up. In fact, I'm sure he wasn't. And listen, they didn't do it just once, either. They've been doing it every two or three weeks for months!'

'And the wives don't know?'

'They haven't a clue.'

'I've got to hear this,' Jerry said. 'Let's get another drink first.'

We crossed to the bar and refilled our glasses, then returned to the sofa.

'You must remember,' I said, 'that there had to be a tremendous lot of preparation and rehearsal beforehand. And many intimate details had to be exchanged to give the plan a chance of working. But the essential part of the scheme was simple:

'They fixed a night, call it Saturday. On that night the husbands and wives were to go up to bed as usual, at say eleven or eleven thirty.

'From then on, normal routine would be preserved. A little reading, perhaps, a little talking, then out with the lights.

'After lights out, the husbands would at once

73

roll over and pretend to go to sleep. This was to discourage their wives from getting fresh, which at this stage must on no account be permitted. So the wives went to sleep. But the husbands stayed awake. So far so good.

'Then at precisely one a.m., by which time the wives would be in a good deep sleep, each husband would slip quietly out of bed, put on a pair of bedroom slippers and creep downstairs in his pyjamas. He would open the front door and go out into the night, taking care not to close the door behind him.

'They lived,' I went on, 'more or less across the street from one another. It was a quiet suburban neighbourhood and there was seldom anyone about at that hour. So these two furtive pyjama-clad figures would pass each other as they crossed the street, each one heading for another house, another bed, another woman.'

Jerry was listening to me carefully. His eyes were a little glazed from drink, but he was listening to every word.

'The next part,' I said, 'had been prepared very thoroughly by both men. Each knew the inside of his friend's house almost as well as he knew his own. He knew how to find his way in the dark both downstairs and up without knocking over the furniture. He knew his way to the stairs and exactly how many steps there were to the top and which of them creaked and which didn't. He knew on which side of the bed the woman upstairs was sleeping.

'Each took off his slippers and left them in the hall, then up the stairs he crept in his bare feet

74

and pyjamas. This part of it, according to my friend, was rather exciting. He was in a dark silent house that wasn't his own, and on his way to the main bedroom he had to pass no less than three children's bedrooms where the doors were always left slightly open.'

'Children!' Jerry cried. 'My God, what if one of them had woken up and said, 'Daddy, is that you?''

'That was all taken care of,' I said. 'Emergency procedure would then come into effect immediately. Also if the wife, just as he was creeping into her room, woke up and said, 'Darling, what's wrong? Why are you wandering about?'; then again, emergency procedure.'

'What emergency procedure?' Jerry said.

'Simple,' I answered. 'The man would immediately dash downstairs and out the front door and across to his own house and ring the bell. This was a signal for the other character, no matter what he was doing at the time, also to rush downstairs at full speed and open the door and let the other fellow in while he went out. This would get them both back quickly to their proper houses.'

'With egg all over their faces,' Jerry said.

'Not at all,' I said.

'That doorbell would have woken the whole house,' Jerry said.

'Of course,' I said. 'And the husband, returning upstairs in his pyjamas, would merely say, 'I went to see who the hell was ringing the bell at this ungodly hour. Couldn't find anyone. It must have been a drunk.''

'What about the other guy?' Jerry asked. 'How does he explain why he rushed downstairs when his wife or child spoke to him?'

'He would say, 'I heard someone prowling about outside, so I rushed down to get him, but he escaped.' 'Did you actually see him?' his wife would ask anxiously. 'Of course I saw him,' the husband would answer. 'He ran off down the street. He was too damn fast for me.' Whereupon the husband would be warmly congratulated for his bravery.'

'Okay,' Jerry said. 'That's the easy part. Everything so far is just a matter of good planning and good timing. But what happens when these two horny characters actually climb into bed with each other's wives?'

'They go right to it,' I said.

'The wives are sleeping,' Jerry said.

'I know,' I said. 'So they proceed immediately with some very gentle but very skilful love-play, and by the time these dames are fully awake, they're as randy as rattlesnakes.'

'No talking, I presume,' Jerry said.

'Not a word.'

'Okay, so the wives are awake,' Jerry said. 'And their hands get to work. So just for a start, what about the simple question of body size? What about the difference between the new man and the husband? What about tallness and shortness and fatness and thinness? You're not telling me these men were physically identical?'

'Not identical, obviously,' I said. 'But they were more or less similar in build and height. That was essential. They were both clean-shaven and had roughly the same amount of hair on their heads. That sort of similarity is commonplace. Look at you and me, for instance. We're roughly the same height and build, aren't we?'

'Are we?' Jerry said.

'How tall are you?' I said.

'Six foot exactly.'

'I'm five eleven,' I said. 'One inch difference. What do you weigh?'

'One hundred and eighty-seven.'

'I'm a hundred and eighty-four,' I said. 'What's three pounds among friends?'

There was a pause. Jerry was looking out through the french windows on to the terrace where my wife, Mary, was standing. Mary was still talking to Bob Swain and the evening sun was shining in her hair. She was a dark pretty girl with a bosom. I watched Jerry. I saw his tongue come out and go sliding along the surface of his lower lip.

'I guess you're right,' Jerry said, still looking at Mary. 'I guess we are about the same size, you and me.' When he turned back and faced me again, there was a little red rose high up on each cheek. 'Go on about these two men,' he said. 'What about some of the other differences?'

'You mean faces?' I said. 'No one's going to see faces in the dark.'

'I'm not talking about faces,' Jerry said.

'What are you talking about, then?'

'I'm talking about their cocks,' Jerry said. 'That's what it's all about, isn't it? And you're not going to tell me . . . '

'Oh yes, I am,' I said. 'Just so long as both men

were either circumcised or uncircumcised, then there was really no problem.'

'Are you seriously suggesting that all men have the same size in cocks?' Jerry said. 'Because they don't.'

'I know they don't,' I said.

'Some are enormous,' Jerry said. 'And some are titchy.'

'There are always exceptions,' I told him. 'But you'd be surprised at the number of men whose measurements are virtually the same, give or take a centimetre. According to my friend, ninety per cent are normal. Only ten per cent are notably large or small.'

'I don't believe that,' Jerry said.

'Check on it sometime,' I said. 'Ask some well-travelled girl.'

Jerry took a long slow sip of his whisky, and his eyes over the top of his glass were looking again at Mary on the terrace. 'What about the rest of it?' he said.

'No problem,' I said.

'No problem, my arse,' he said. 'Shall I tell you why this is a phony story?'

'Go ahead.'

'Everybody knows that a wife and husband who have been married for some years develop a kind of routine. It's inevitable. My God, a new operator would be spotted instantly. You know damn well he would. You can't suddenly wade in with a totally different style and expect the woman not to notice it, and I don't care how randy she was. She'd smell a rat in the first minute!'

78

'A routine can be duplicated,' I said. 'Just so long as every detail of that routine is described beforehand.'

'A bit personal, that,' Jerry said.

'The whole thing's personal,' I said. 'So each man tells his story. He tells precisely what he usually does. He tells everything. The lot. The works. The whole routine from beginning to end.'

'Jesus,' Jerry said.

'Each of these men,' I said, 'had to learn a new part. He had, in effect, to become an actor. He was impersonating another character.'

'Not so easy, that,' Jerry said.

'No problem at all, according to my friend. The only thing one had to watch out for was not to get carried away and start improvising. One had to follow the stage directions very carefully and stick to them.'

Jerry took another pull at his drink. He also took another look at Mary on the terrace. Then he leaned back against the sofa, glass in hand.

'These two characters,' he said. 'You mean they actually pulled it off?'

'I'm damn sure they did,' I said. 'They're still doing it. About once every three weeks.'

'Fantastic story,' Jerry said. 'And a damn crazy dangerous thing to do. Just imagine the sort of hell that would break loose if you were caught. Instant divorce. Two divorces, in fact. One on each side of the street. Not worth it.'

'Takes a lot of guts,' I said.

'The party's breaking up,' Jerry said. 'They're all going home with their goddamn wives.'

I didn't say any more after that. We sat there

79

for a couple of minutes sipping our drinks while the guests began drifting towards the hall.

'Did he say it was fun, this friend of yours?' Jerry asked suddenly.

'He said it was a gas,' I answered. 'He said all the normal pleasures got intensified one hundred per cent because of the risk. He swore it was the greatest way of doing it in the world, impersonating the husband and the wife not knowing it.'

At that point, Mary came in through the french windows with Bob Swain. She had an empty glass in one hand and a flame-coloured azalea in the other. She had picked the azalea on the terrace.

'I've been watching you,' she said, pointing the flower at me like a pistol. 'You've hardly stopped talking for the last ten minutes. What's he been telling you, Jerry?'

'A dirty story,' Jerry said, grinning.

'He does that when he drinks,' Mary said.

'Good story,' Jerry said. 'But totally impossible. Get him to tell it to you sometime.'

'I don't like dirty stories,' Mary said. 'Come along, Vic. It's time we went.'

'Don't go yet,' Jerry said, fixing his eyes upon her splendid bosom. 'Have another drink.'

'No thanks,' she said. 'The children'll be screaming for their supper. I've had a lovely time.'

'Aren't you going to kiss me good night?' Jerry said, getting up from the sofa. He went for her mouth, but she turned her head quickly and he caught only the edge of her cheek.

'Go away, Jerry,' she said. 'You're drunk.'

'Not drunk,' Jerry said. 'Just lecherous.'

'Don't you get lecherous with me, my boy,' Mary said sharply. 'I hate that sort of talk.' She marched away across the room, carrying her bosom before her like a battering-ram.

'So long, Jerry,' I said. 'Fine party.'

Mary, full of dark looks, was waiting for me in the hall. Samantha was there, too, saying goodbye to the last guests — Samantha with her dexterous fingers and her smooth skin and her smooth, dangerous thighs. 'Cheer up, Vic,' she said to me, her white teeth showing. She looked like the creation, the beginning of the world, the first morning. 'Good night, Vic darling,' she said, stirring her fingers in my vitals.

I followed Mary out of the house. 'You feeling all right?' she asked.

'Yes,' I said. 'Why not?'

'The amount you drink is enough to make anyone feel ill,' she said.

There was a scrubby old hedge dividing our place from Jerry's and there was a gap in it we always used. Mary and I walked through the gap in silence. We went into the house and she cooked up a big pile of scrambled eggs and bacon, and we ate it with the children.

After the meal, I wandered outside. The summer evening was clear and cool and because I had nothing else to do I decided to mow the grass in the front garden. I got the mower out of the shed and started it up. Then I began the old routine of marching back and forth behind it. I like mowing grass. It is a soothing operation, and on our front lawn I could always look at Samantha's house going one way and think about her going the other.

I had been at it for about ten minutes when Jerry came strolling through the gap in the hedge. He was smoking a pipe and had his hands in his pockets and he stood on the edge of the grass, watching me. I pulled up in front of him, but left the motor ticking over.

'Hi, sport,' he said. 'How's everything?'

'I'm in the doghouse,' I said. 'So are you.'

'Your little wife,' he said, 'is just too goddamn prim and prissy to be true.'

'Oh, I know that.'

'She rebuked me in my own house,' Jerry said.

'Not very much.'

'It was enough,' he said, smiling slightly.

'Enough for what?'

'Enough to make me want to get a little bit of my own back on her. So what would you think if I suggested you and I have a go at that thing your friend told you about at lunch?'

When he said this, I felt such a surge of excitement my stomach nearly jumped out of my mouth. I gripped the handles of the mower and started revving the engine.

'Have I said the wrong thing?' Jerry asked.

I didn't answer.

'Listen,' he said. 'If you think it's a lousy idea, let's just forget I ever mentioned it. You're not mad at me, are you?'

'I'm not mad at you, Jerry,' I said. 'It's just that it never entered my head that we should do it.'

'It entered mine,' he said. 'The set-up is perfect. We wouldn't even have to cross the street.'

His face had gone suddenly bright and his eyes were shining like two stars. 'So what do you say, Vic?'

'I'm thinking,' I said.

'Maybe you don't fancy Samantha.'

'I don't honestly know,' I said.

'She's lots of fun,' Jerry said. 'I guarantee that.'

At this point, I saw Mary come out on to the front porch. 'There's Mary,' I said. 'She's looking for the children. We'll talk some more tomorrow.'

'Then it's a deal?'

'It could be, Jerry. But only on condition we don't rush it. I want to be dead sure everything is right before we start. Damn it all, this is a whole brand-new can of beans!'

'No, it's not!' he said. 'Your friend said it was a gas. He said it was easy.'

'Ah, yes,' I said. 'My friend. Of course. But each case is different.' I opened the throttle on the mower and went whirring away across the lawn. When I got to the far side and turned around, Jerry was already through the gap in the hedge and walking up to his front door.

The next couple of weeks was a period of high conspiracy for Jerry and me. We held secret meetings in bars and restaurants to discuss strategy, and sometimes he dropped into my office after work and we had a planning session behind the closed door. Whenever a doubtful point arose, Jerry would always say, 'How did your friend do it?' And I would play for time and say, 'I'll call him up and ask him about that one.'

After many conferences and much talk, we agreed upon the following main points:

1. That D Day should be a Saturday.
2. That on D Day evening we should take our wives out to a good dinner, the four of us together.
3. That Jerry and I should leave our houses and cross over through the gap in the hedge at precisely one a.m. Sunday morning.
4. That instead of lying in bed in the dark until one a.m. came along, we should both, as soon as our wives were asleep, go quietly downstairs to the kitchen and drink coffee.
5. That we should use the front doorbell idea if an emergency arose.
6. That the return cross-over time was fixed for two a.m.
7. That while in the wrong bed, questions (if any) from the woman must be answered by an 'Uh-uh' sounded with the lips closed tight.
8. That I myself must immediately give up cigarettes and take to a pipe so that I would 'smell' the same as Jerry.
9. That we should at once start using the same brand of hair oil and after-shave lotion.
10. That as both of us normally wore our wrist-watches in bed, and they were much the same shape, it was decided not to exchange. Neither of us wore rings.
11. That each man must have something unusual about him that the woman

would identify positively with her own husband. We therefore invented what became known as 'The Sticking Plaster Ploy'. It worked like this: on D Day evening, when the couples arrived back in their own homes immediately after the dinner, each husband would make a point of going to the kitchen to cut himself a piece of cheese. At the same time, he would carefully stick a large piece of plaster over the tip of the forefinger of his right hand. Having done this, he would hold up the finger and say to his wife, 'I cut myself. It's nothing, but it was bleeding a bit.' Thus, later on, when the men have switched beds, each woman will be made very much aware of the plaster-covered finger (the man would see to that), and will associate it directly with her own husband. An important psychological ploy, this, calculated to dissipate any tiny suspicion that might enter the mind of either female.

So much for the basic plans. Next came what we referred to in our notes as 'Familiarization with the Layout'. Jerry schooled me first. He gave me three hours' training in his own house one Sunday afternoon when his wife and children were out. I had never been into their bedroom before. On the dressing table were Samantha's perfumes, her brushes, and all her other little things. A pair of her stockings was draped over the back of a chair. Her nightdress, white and blue, was hanging behind the door leading to the bathroom.

'Okay,' Jerry said. 'It'll be pitch dark when you come in. Samantha sleeps on this side, so you must tiptoe around the end of the bed and slide in on the other side, over there. I'm going to blindfold you and let you practise.'

At first, with the blindfold on, I wandered all over the room like a drunk. But after about an hour's work, I was able to negotiate the course pretty well. But before Jerry would finally pass me out, I had to go blindfold all the way from the front door through the hall, up the stairs, past the children's rooms, into Samantha's room and finish up in exactly the right place. And I had to do it silently, like a thief. All this took three hours of hard work, but I got it in the end.

The following Sunday morning when Mary had taken our children to church, I was able to give Jerry the same sort of work-out in my house. He learned the ropes faster than me, and within an hour he had passed the blindfold test without placing a foot wrong.

It was during this session that we decided to disconnect each woman's bedside lamp as we entered the bedroom. So Jerry practised finding the plug and pulling it out with his blindfold on, and the following week-end, I was able to do the same in Jerry's house.

Now came by far the most important part of our training. We called it 'Spilling the Beans', and it was here that both of us had to describe in

86

every detail the procedure we adopted when making love to our own wives. We agreed not to worry ourselves with any exotic variations that either of us might or might not occasionally practise. We were concerned only with teaching one another the most commonly used routine, the one least likely to arouse suspicion.

The session took place in my office at six o'clock on a Wednesday evening, after the staff had gone home. At first, we were both slightly embarrassed, and neither of us wanted to begin. So I got out the bottle of whisky, and after a couple of stiff drinks, we loosened up and the teach-in started. While Jerry talked I took notes, and vice versa. At the end of it all, it turned out that the only real difference between Jerry's routine and my own was one of tempo. But what a difference it was! He took things (if what he said was to be believed) in such a leisurely fashion and he prolonged the moments to such an extravagant degree that I wondered privately to myself whether his partner did not sometimes go to sleep in the middle of it all. My job, however, was not to criticize but to copy, and I said nothing.

Jerry was not so discreet. At the end of my personal description, he had the temerity to say, 'Is that really what you do?'

'What do you mean?' I asked.

'I mean is it all over and done with as quickly as that?'

'Look,' I said. 'We aren't here to give each other lessons. We're here to learn the facts.'

'I know that,' he said. 'But I'm going to feel a

bit of an ass if I copy your style exactly. My God, you go through it like an express train whizzing through a country station!'

I stared at him, mouth open.

'Don't look so surprised,' he said. 'The way you told it to me, anyone would think . . . '

'Think what?' I said.

'Oh, forget it,' he said.

'Thank you,' I said. I was furious. There are two things in this world at which I happen to know I excel. One is driving an automobile and the other is you-know-what. So to have him sit there and tell me I didn't know how to behave with my own wife was a monstrous piece of effrontery. It was he who didn't know, not me. Poor Samantha. What she must have had to put up with over the years.

'I'm sorry I spoke,' Jerry said. He poured more whisky into our glasses. 'Here's to the great switcheroo!' he said. 'When do we go?'

'Today is Wednesday,' I said. 'How about this coming Saturday?'

'Christ,' Jerry said.

'We ought to do it while everything's still fresh in our minds,' I said. 'There's an awful lot to remember.'

Jerry walked to the window and looked down at the traffic in the street below. 'Okay,' he said, turning around. 'Next Saturday it shall be!' Then we drove home in our separate cars.

'Jerry and I thought we'd take you and Samantha out to dinner Saturday night,' I said to Mary. We were in the kitchen and she was cooking hamburgers for the children.

She turned around and faced me, frying-pan in one hand, spoon in the other. Her blue eyes looked straight into mine. 'My Lord, Vic,' she said. 'How nice. But what are we celebrating?'

I looked straight back at her and said, 'I thought it would be a change to see some new faces. We're always meeting the same old bunch of people in the same old houses.'

She took a step forward and kissed me on the cheek. 'What a good man you are,' she said. 'I love you.'

'Don't forget to phone the baby-sitter.'

'No, I'll do it tonight,' she said.

Thursday and Friday passed very quickly, and suddenly it was Saturday. It was D Day. I woke up feeling madly excited. After breakfast, I couldn't sit still, so I decided to go out and wash the car. I was in the middle of this when Jerry came strolling through the gap in the hedge, pipe in mouth.

'Hi, sport,' he said. 'This is the day.'

'I know that,' I said. I also had a pipe in my mouth. I was forcing myself to smoke it, but I had trouble keeping it alight, and the smoke burned my tongue.

'How're you feeling?' Jerry asked.

'Terrific,' I said. 'How about you?'

'I'm nervous,' he said.

'Don't be nervous, Jerry.'

'This is one hell of a thing we're trying to do,' he said. 'I hope we pull it off.'

I went on polishing the windshield. I had never known Jerry to be nervous of anything before. It worried me a bit.

'I'm damn glad we're not the first people ever to try it,' he said. 'If no one had ever done it before, I don't think I'd risk it.'

'I agree,' I said.

'What stops me being too nervous,' he said, 'is the fact that your friend found it so fantastically easy.'

'My friend said it was a cinch,' I said. 'But for Chrissake, Jerry, don't be nervous when the time comes. That would be disastrous.'

'Don't worry,' he said. 'But Jesus, it's exciting, isn't it?'

'It's exciting all right,' I said.

'Listen,' he said. 'We'd better go easy on the booze tonight.'

'Good idea,' I said. 'See you at eight thirty.'

At half past eight, Samantha, Jerry, Mary, and I drove in Jerry's car to Billy's Steak House. The restaurant, despite its name, was high-class and expensive, and the girls had put on long dresses for the occasion. Samantha was wearing something green that didn't start until it was halfway down her front, and I had never seen her looking lovelier. There were candles on our table. Samantha was seated opposite me and whenever she leaned forward with her face close to the flame, I could see that tiny crest of skin at the top centre of her lower lip. 'Now,' she said as she accepted a menu from the waiter, 'I wonder what I'm going to have tonight.'

Ho-ho-ho, I thought, that's a good question.

Everything went fine in the restaurant and the girls enjoyed themselves. When we arrived back at Jerry's house, it was eleven forty-five, and

90

Samantha said, 'Come in and have a nightcap.'

'Thanks,' I said, 'but it's a bit late. And the baby-sitter has to be driven home.' So Mary and I walked across to our house, and *now*, I told myself as I entered the front door, *from now on* the countdown begins. I must keep a clear head and forget nothing.

While Mary was paying the baby-sitter, I went to the fridge and found a piece of Canadian cheddar. I took a knife from the drawer and a strip of plaster from the cupboard. I stuck the plaster around the tip of the forefinger of my right hand and waited for Mary to turn around.

'I cut myself,' I said holding up the finger for her to see. 'It's nothing, but it was bleeding a bit.'

'I'd have thought you'd had enough to eat for the evening,' was all she said. But the plaster registered on her mind and my first little job had been done.

I drove the baby-sitter home and by the time I got back up to the bedroom it was round about midnight and Mary was already half asleep with her light out. I switched out the light on my side of the bed and went into the bathroom to undress. I pottered about in there for ten minutes or so and when I came out, Mary, as I had hoped, was well and truly sleeping. There seemed no point in getting into bed beside her. So I simply pulled back the covers a bit on my side to make it easier for Jerry, then with my slippers on, I went downstairs to the kitchen and switched on the electric kettle. It was now twelve seventeen. Forty-three minutes to go.

At twelve thirty-five, I went upstairs to check on Mary and the kids. Everyone was sound asleep.

At twelve fifty-five, five minutes before zero hour, I went up again for a final check. I went right up close to Mary's bed and whispered her name. There was no answer. Good. *That's it! Let's go!*

I put a brown raincoat over my pyjamas. I switched off the kitchen light so that the whole house was in darkness. I put the front door lock on the latch. And then, feeling an enormous sense of exhilaration, I stepped silently out into the night.

There were no lamps on our street to lighten the darkness. There was no moon or even a star to be seen. It was a black black night, but the air was warm and there was a little breeze blowing from somewhere.

I headed for the gap in the hedge. When I got very close, I was able to make out the hedge itself and find the gap. I stopped there, waiting. Then I heard Jerry's footsteps coming toward me.

'Hi, sport,' he whispered. 'Everything okay?'

'All ready for you,' I whispered back.

He moved on. I heard his slippered feet padding softly over the grass as he went toward my house. I went toward his.

I opened Jerry's front door. It was even darker inside than out. I closed the door carefully. I took off my raincoat and hung it on the door knob. I removed my slippers and placed them against the wall by the door. I literally could not see my hands before my face. Everything had to be done by touch.

My goodness, I was glad Jerry had made me practise blindfold for so long. It wasn't my feet that guided me now but my fingers. The fingers of one hand or another were never for a moment out of contact with something, a wall, the banister, a piece of furniture, a window-curtain. And I knew or thought I knew exactly where I was all the time. But it was an awesome eerie feeling trespassing on tiptoe through someone else's house in the middle of the night. As I fingered my way up the stairs, I found myself thinking of the burglars who had broken into our front room last winter and stolen the television set. When the police came next morning, I pointed out to them an enormous turd lying in the snow outside the garage. 'They nearly always do that,' one of the cops told me. 'They can't help it. They're scared.'

I reached the top of the stairs. I crossed the landing with my right fingertips touching the wall all the time. I started down the corridor, but paused when my hand found the door of the first children's room. The door was slightly open. I listened. I could hear young Robert Rainbow, aged eight, breathing evenly inside. I moved on. I found the door to the second children's bedroom. This one belonged to Billy, aged six and Amanda, three. I stood listening. All was well.

The main bedroom was at the end of the corridor, about four yards on. I reached the door. Jerry had left it open, as planned. I went in.

I stood absolutely still just inside the door, listening for any sign that Samantha might be awake. All was quiet. I felt my way around the wall until I reached Samantha's side of the bed. Immediately, I knelt on the floor and found the plug connecting her bedside lamp. I drew it from its socket and laid it on the carpet. Good. Much safer now. I stood up. I couldn't see Samantha, and at first I couldn't hear anything either. I bent low over the bed. Ah yes, I could hear her breathing. Suddenly I caught a whiff of the heavy musky perfume she had been using that evening, and I felt the blood rushing to my groin. Quickly I tiptoed around the big bed, keeping two fingers in gentle contact with the edge of the bed the whole way.

All I had to do now was get in. I did so, but as I put my weight upon the mattress, the creaking of the springs underneath sounded as though someone was firing a rifle in the room. I lay motionless, holding my breath. I could hear my heart thumping away like an engine in my throat. Samantha was facing away from me. She didn't move. I pulled the covers up over my chest and turned toward her. A female glow came out of her to me. Here we go, then! *Now!*

I slid a hand over and touched her body. Her nightdress was warm and silky. I rested the hand gently on her hips. Still she didn't move. I waited a minute or so, then I allowed the hand that lay upon the hip to steal onward and go exploring. Slowly, deliberately, and very accurately, my fingers began the process of setting her on fire.

She stirred. She turned on to her back. Then

she murmured sleepily, 'Oh, dear . . . Oh, my goodness me . . . Good heavens, darling!'

I, of course, said nothing. I just kept on with the job.

A couple of minutes went by.

She was lying quite still.

Another minute passed. Then another. She didn't move a muscle.

I began to wonder how much longer it would be before she caught alight.

I persevered.

But why the silence? Why this absolute and total immobility, this frozen posture?

Suddenly it came to me. I had forgotten completely about Jerry! I was so hotted up, I had forgotten all about his own personal routine! I was doing it my way, not his! His way was far more complex than mine. It was ridiculously elaborate. It was quite unnecessary. But it was what she was used to. And now she was noticing the difference and trying to figure out what on earth was going on.

But it was too late to change direction now. I must keep going.

I kept going. The woman beside me was like a coiled spring lying there. I could feel the tension under her skin. I began to sweat.

Suddenly, she uttered a queer little groan.

More ghastly thoughts rushed through my mind. Could she be ill? Was she having a heart attack? Ought I to get the hell out quick?

She groaned again, louder this time. Then all at once, she cried out, 'Yes-yes-yes-yes-yes!' and like a bomb whose slow fuse had finally reached

95

the dynamite, she exploded into life. She grabbed me in her arms and went for me with such incredible ferocity, I felt I was being set upon by a tiger.

Or should I say tigress?

I never dreamed a woman could do the things Samantha did to me then. She was a whirlwind, a dazzling frenzied whirlwind that tore me up by the roots and spun me around and carried me high into the heavens, to places I did not know existed.

I myself did not contribute. How could I? I was helpless. I was the palm-tree spinning in the heavens, the lamb in the claws of the tiger. It was as much as I could do to keep breathing.

Thrilling it was, all the same, to surrender to the hands of a violent woman, and for the next ten, twenty, thirty minutes — how would I know? — the storm raged on. But I have no intention here of regaling the reader with bizarre details. I do not approve of washing juicy linen in public. I am sorry, but there it is. I only hope that my reticence will not create too strong a sense of anticlimax. Certainly, there was nothing anti about my own climax, and in the final searing paroxysm I gave a shout which should have awakened the entire neighbourhood. Then I collapsed. I crumpled up like a drained wineskin.

Samantha, as though she had done no more than drink a glass of water, simply turned away from me and went right back to sleep.

Phew!

I lay still, recuperating slowly.

I had been right, you see, about that little

thing on her lower lip, had I not?

Come to think of it, I had been right about more or less everything that had to do with this incredible escapade. What a triumph! I felt wonderfully relaxed and well-spent.

I wondered what time it was. My watch was not a luminous one. I'd better go. I crept out of bed. I felt my way, a trifle less cautiously this time, around the bed, out of the bedroom, along the corridor, down the stairs and into the hall of the house. I found my raincoat and slippers. I put them on. I had a lighter in the pocket of my raincoat. I used it and read the time. It was eight minutes before two. Later than I thought, I opened the front door and stepped out into the black night.

My thoughts now began to concentrate upon Jerry. Was he all right? Had he gotten away with it? I moved through the darkness toward the gap in the hedge.

'Hi, sport,' a voice whispered beside me.

'Jerry!'

'Everything okay?' Jerry asked.

'Fantastic,' I said. 'Amazing. What about you?'

'Same with me,' he said. I caught the flash of his white teeth grinning at me in the dark. 'We made it, Vic!' he whispered, touching my arm. 'You were right! It worked! It was sensational!'

'See you tomorrow,' I whispered. 'Go home.'

We moved apart. I went through the hedge and entered my house. Three minutes later, I was safely back in my own bed, and my own wife was sleeping soundly alongside me.

The next morning was Sunday. I was up at

eight thirty and went downstairs in pyjamas and
dressing-gown, as I always do on a Sunday, to
make breakfast for the family. I had left Mary
sleeping. The two boys, Victor, aged nine, and
Wally, seven, were already down.

'Hi, daddy,' Wally said.

'I've got a great new breakfast,' I announced.

'What?' both boys said together. They had
been into town and fetched the Sunday paper
and were now reading the comics.

'We make some buttered toast and we spread
orange marmalade on it,' I said. 'Then we put
strips of crisp bacon on top of the marmalade.'

'*Bacon!*' Victor said. 'With *orange marmalade!*'

'I know. But you wait till you try it. It's
wonderful.'

I dished out the grapefruit juice and drank two
glasses of it myself. I set another on the table for
Mary when she came down. I switched on the
electric kettle, put the bread in the toaster, and
started to fry the bacon. At this point, Mary
came into the kitchen. She had a flimsy
peach-coloured chiffon thing over her nightdress.

'Good morning,' I said, watching her over my
shoulder as I manipulated the frying-pan.

She did not answer. She went to her chair at
the kitchen table and sat down. She started to
sip her juice. She looked neither at me nor at the
boys. I went on frying the bacon.

'Hi, mummy,' Wally said.

She didn't answer this either.

The smell of the bacon fat was beginning to
turn my stomach.

'I'd like some coffee,' Mary said, not looking around. Her voice was very odd.

'Coming right up,' I said. I pushed the frying-pan away from the heat and quickly made a cup of black instant coffee. I placed it before her.

'Boys,' she said, addressing the children, 'would you please do your reading in the other room till breakfast is ready.'

'Us?' Victor said. 'Why?'

'Because I say so.'

'Are we doing something wrong?' Wally asked.

'No, honey, you're not. I just want to be left alone for a moment with daddy.'

I felt myself shrink inside my skin. I wanted to run. I wanted to rush out the front door and go running down the street and hide.

'Get yourself a coffee, Vic,' she said, 'and sit down.' Her voice was quite flat. There was no anger in it. There was just nothing. And she still wouldn't look at me. The boys went out, taking the comic section with them.

'Shut the door,' Mary said to them.

I put a spoonful of powdered coffee into my cup and poured boiling water over it. I added milk and sugar. The silence was shattering. I crossed over and sat down in my chair opposite her. It might just as well have been an electric chair, the way I was feeling.

'Listen, Vic,' she said, looking into her coffee cup. 'I want to get this said before I lose my nerve and then I won't be able to say it.'

'For heaven's sake, what's all the drama about?' I asked. 'Has something happened?'

99

'Yes, Vic, it has.'

'What?'

Her face was pale and still and distant, unconscious of the kitchen around her.

'Come on, then, out with it,' I said bravely.

'You're not going to like this very much,' she said, and her big blue haunted-looking eyes rested a moment on my face, then travelled away.

'What am I not going to like very much?' I said. The sheer terror of it all was beginning to stir my bowels. I felt the same way as those burglars the cops had told me about.

'You know I hate talking about love-making and all that sort of thing,' she said. 'I've never once talked to you about it all the time we've been married.'

'That's true,' I said.

She took a sip of her coffee, but she wasn't tasting it. 'The point is this,' she said. 'I've never liked it. If you really want to know, I've hated it.'

'Hated what?' I asked.

'Sex,' she said. 'Doing it.'

'Good Lord!' I said.

'It's never given me even the slightest little bit of pleasure.'

This was shattering enough in itself, but the real cruncher was still to come, I felt sure of that.

'I'm sorry if that surprises you,' she added.

I couldn't think of anything to say, so I kept quiet.

Her eyes rose again from the coffee cup and looked into mine, watchful, as if calculating something, then fell again. 'I wasn't ever going to tell you,' she said. 'And I never would have if it hadn't been for last night.'

I said very slowly, 'What about last night?'

'Last night,' she said, 'I suddenly found out what the whole crazy thing is all about.'

'You did?'

She looked full at me now, and her face was as open as a flower. 'Yes,' she said. 'I surely did.'

I didn't move.

'Oh darling!' she cried, jumping up and rushing over and giving me an enormous kiss. 'Thank you so much for last night! You were marvellous! And I was marvellous! We were both marvellous! Don't look so embarrassed, my darling! You ought to be proud of yourself! You were fantastic! I love you! I do! I do!'

I just sat there.

She leaned close to me and put an arm around my shoulders. 'And now,' she said softly, 'now that you have . . . I don't quite know how to say this . . . now that you have sort of discovered what it is I *need*, everything is going to be so marvellous from now on!'

I still sat there. She went slowly back to her chair. A big tear was running down one of her cheeks. I couldn't think why.

'I was right to tell you, wasn't I?' she said, smiling through her tears.

'Yes,' I said. 'Oh, yes.' I stood up and went over to the cooker so that I wouldn't be facing her. Through the kitchen window, I caught sight of Jerry crossing his garden with the Sunday paper under his arm. There was a lilt in his walk,

101

a little prance of triumph in each pace he took, and when he reached the steps of his front porch, he ran up them two at a time.

The Last Act

Anna was in the kitchen washing a head of Boston lettuce for the family supper when the doorbell rang. The bell itself was on the wall directly above the sink, and it never failed to make her jump if it rang when she happened to be near. For this reason, neither her husband nor any of the children ever used it. It seemed to ring extra loud this time, and Anna jumped extra high.

When she opened the door, two policemen were standing outside. They looked at her out of pale waxen faces, and she looked back at them, waiting for them to say something.

She kept looking at them, but they didn't speak or move. They stood so still and so rigid that they were like two wax figures somebody had put on her doorstep as a joke. Each of them was holding his helmet in front of him in his two hands.

'What is it?' Anna asked.

They were both young, and they were wearing leather gauntlets up to their elbows. She could see their enormous motor-cycles propped up along the edge of the sidewalk behind them, and dead leaves were falling around the motor-cycles and blowing along the sidewalk and the whole of the street was brilliant in the yellow light of a clear, gusty September evening. The taller of the two policemen shifted uneasily on his feet. Then he said quietly, 'Are you Mrs Cooper, ma'am?'

'Yes, I am.'

The other said, 'Mrs Edmund J. Cooper?'

'Yes.' And then slowly it began to dawn upon her that these men, neither of whom seemed anxious to explain his presence, would not be behaving as they were unless they had some distasteful duty to perform.

'Mrs Cooper,' she heard one of them saying, and from the way he said it, as gently and softly as if he were comforting a sick child, she knew at once that he was going to tell her something terrible. A great wave of panic came over her, and she said, 'What happened?'

'We have to inform you, Mrs Cooper . . . '

The policeman paused, and the woman, watching him, felt as though her whole body were shrinking and shrinking and shrinking inside its skin.

' . . . that your husband was involved in an accident on the Hudson River Parkway at approximately five forty-five this evening, and died in the ambulance . . . '

The policeman who was speaking produced the crocodile wallet she had given Ed on their twentieth wedding anniversary, two years back, and as she reached out to take it, she found herself wondering whether it might not still be warm from having been close to her husband's chest only a short while ago.

'If there's anything we can do,' the policeman was saying, 'like calling up somebody to come over . . . some friend or relative maybe . . . '

Anna heard his voice drifting away, then

fading out altogether, and it must have been about then that she began to scream. Soon she became hysterical, and the two policemen had their hands full trying to control her until the doctor arrived some forty minutes later and injected something into her arm.

She was no better, though, when she woke up the following morning. Neither her doctor nor her children were able to reason with her in any way at all, and had she not been kept under almost constant sedation for the next few days, she would undoubtedly have taken her own life. In the brief lucid periods between drug-takings, she acted as though she were demented, calling out her husband's name and telling him that she was coming to join him as soon as she possibly could. It was terrible to listen to her. But in defence of her behaviour, it should be said at once that this was no ordinary husband she had lost.

Anna Greenwood had married Ed Cooper when they were both eighteen, and over the time they were together, they grew to be closer and more dependent upon each other than it is possible to describe in words. Every year that went by, their love became more intense and overwhelming, and toward the end, it had reached such a ridiculous peak that it was almost impossible for them to endure the daily separation caused by Ed's departure for the office in the mornings. When he returned at night he would rush through the house to seek her out, and she, who had heard the noise of the front door slamming, would drop everything and rush simultaneously in his direction, meeting him head on, recklessly, at full speed, perhaps halfway up the stairs, or on the landing, or between the kitchen and the hall; and as they came together, he would take her in his arms and hug her and kiss her for minutes on end as though she were yesterday's bride. It was wonderful. It was so utterly unbelievably wonderful that one is very nearly able to understand why she should have had no desire and no heart to continue living in a world where her husband did not exist any more.

Her three children, Angela (twenty), Mary (nineteen) and Billy (seventeen and a half), stayed around her constantly right from the start of the catastrophe. They adored their mother, and they certainly had no intention of letting her commit suicide if they could help it. They worked hard and with loving desperation to convince her that life could still be worth living, and it was due entirely to them that she managed in the end to come out of the nightmare and climb back slowly into the ordinary world.

Four months after the disaster, she was pronounced 'moderately safe' by the doctors, and she was able to return, albeit rather listlessly, to the old routine of running the house and doing the shopping and cooking the meals for her grown-up children.

But then what happened?

Before the snows of that winter had melted away, Angela married a young man from Rhode Island and went off to live in the suburbs of Providence.

106

A few months later, Mary married a fair-haired giant from a town called Slayton, in Minnesota, and away she flew for ever and ever and ever. And although Anna's heart was now beginning to break all over again into tiny pieces, she was proud to think that neither of the two girls had the slightest inkling of what was happening to her. ('Oh, Mummy, isn't it wonderful!' 'Yes, my darling, I think it's the most beautiful wedding there's ever been! I'm even more excited than you are!' etc. etc.)

And then, to put the lid on everything, her beloved Billy, who had just turned eighteen, went off to begin his first year at Yale.

So all at once, Anna found herself living in a completely empty house.

It is an awful feeling, after twenty-three years of boisterous, busy, magical family life, to come down alone to breakfast in the mornings, to sit there in silence with a cup of coffee and a piece of toast, and to wonder what you are going to do with the day that lies ahead. The room you are sitting in, which has heard so much laughter, and seen so many birthdays, so many Christmas trees, so many presents being opened, is quiet now and feels curiously cold. The air is heated and the temperature itself is normal, but the place still makes you shiver. The clock has stopped because you were never the one who wound it in the first place. A chair stands crooked on its legs, and you sit staring at it, wondering why you hadn't noticed it before. And when you glance up again, you have a sudden panicky feeling that all the four walls of the room have begun creeping in upon you very very slowly when you weren't looking.

In the beginning, she would carry her coffee cup over to the telephone and start calling up friends. But all her friends had husbands and children, and although they were always as nice and warm and cheerful as they could possibly be, they simply could not spare the time to sit and chat with a desolate lady from across the way first thing in the morning. So then she started calling up her married daughters instead.

They, also, were sweet and kind to her at all times, but Anna detected, very soon, a subtle change in their attitudes toward her. She was no longer number one in their lives. They had husbands now, and were concentrating everything upon them. Gently but firmly, they were moving their mother into the background. It was quite a shock. But she knew they were right. They were absolutely right. She was no longer entitled to impinge upon their lives or to make them feel guilty for neglecting her.

She saw Dr Jacobs regularly, but he wasn't really any help. He tried to get her to talk and she did her best, and sometimes he made little speeches to her full of oblique remarks about sex and sublimation. Anna never properly understood what he was driving at, but the burden of his song appeared to be that she should get herself another man.

She took to wandering around the house and fingering things that used to belong to Ed. She would pick up one of his shoes and put her hand into it and feel the little dents that the ball of his

108

foot and his toes had made upon the sole. She found a sock with a hole in it, and the pleasure it gave her to darn that sock was indescribable. Occasionally, she took out a shirt, a tie, and a suit, and laid them on the bed, all ready for him to wear, and once, one rainy Sunday morning, she made an Irish stew . . .

It was hopeless to go on.

So how many pills would she need to make absolutely sure of it this time? She went upstairs to her secret store and counted them. There were only nine. Was that enough? She doubted that it was. Oh, hell. The one thing she was not prepared to face all over again was failure — the rush to the hospital, the stomach-pump, the seventh floor of the Payne Whitney Pavilion, the psychiatrists, the humiliation, the misery of it all . . .

In that case, it would have to be the razor-blade. But the trouble with the razor-blade was that it had to be done properly. Many people failed miserably when they tried to use the razor-blade on the wrist. In fact, nearly all of them failed. They didn't cut deep enough. There was a big artery down there somewhere that simply had to be reached. Veins were no good. Veins made plenty of mess, but they never quite managed to do the trick. Then again, the razor-blade was not an easy thing to hold, not if one had to make a firm incision, pressing it right home all the way, deep deep down. But *she* wouldn't fail. The ones who failed were the ones who actually *wanted* to fail. She wanted to succeed.

She went to the cupboard in the bathroom, searching for blades. There weren't any. Ed's razor was still there, and so was hers. But there was no blade in either of them, and no little packet lying alongside. That was understandable. Such things had been removed from the house on an earlier occasion. But there was no problem. Anyone could buy a packet of razor-blades.

She returned to the kitchen and took the calendar down from the wall. She chose September 23rd, which was Ed's birthday, and wrote r-b (for razor-blades) against the date. She did this on September 9th, which gave her exactly two weeks' grace to put her affairs in order. There was much to be done — old bills to be paid, a new will to be written, the house to be tidied up, Billy's college fees to be taken care of for the next four years, letters to the children, to her own parents, to Ed's mother, and so on and so forth.

Yet, busy as she was, she found that those two weeks, those fourteen long days, were going far too slowly for her liking. She wanted to use the blade, and eagerly every morning she counted the days that were left. She was like a child counting the days before Christmas. For wherever it was that Ed Cooper had gone when he died, even if it were only to the grave, she was impatient to join him.

It was in the middle of this two-week period that her friend Elizabeth Paoletti came calling on her at eight thirty one morning. Anna was making coffee in the kitchen at the time, and she

110

jumped when the bell rang and jumped again when it gave a second long blast.

Liz came sweeping in through the front door, talking nonstop as usual. 'Anna, my darling woman, I need your help! Everyone's down with flu at the office. You've *got* to come! Don't argue with me! I know you can type and I know you haven't got a damn thing in the world to do all day except mope. Just grab your hat and purse and let's get going. Hurry up, girl, hurry up! I'm late as it is!'

Anna said, 'Go away, Liz. Leave me alone.'

'The cab is waiting,' Liz said.

'Please,' Anna said, 'don't try to bully me now. I'm not coming.'

'You are coming,' Liz said. 'Pull yourself together. Your days of glorious martyrdom are over.'

Anna continued to resist, but Liz wore her down, and in the end she agreed to go along just for a few hours.

Elizabeth Paoletti was in charge of an adoption society, one of the best in the city. Nine of the staff were down with flu. Only two were left, excluding herself. 'You don't know a thing about the work,' she said in the cab, 'but you're just going to have to help us all you can . . .'

The office was bedlam. The telephones alone nearly drove Anna mad. She kept running from one cubicle to the next, taking messages that she did not understand. And there were girls in the waiting room, young girls with ashen stony faces, and it became part of her duty to type their answers on an official form.

'The father's name?'

'Don't know.'

'You've no idea?'

'What's the father's name got to do with it?'

'My dear, if the father is known, then his consent has to be obtained as well as yours before the child can be offered for adoption.'

'You're quite sure about that?'

'Jesus, I told you, didn't I?'

At lunchtime, somebody brought her a sandwich, but there was no time to eat it. At nine o'clock that night, exhausted and famished and considerably shaken by some of the knowledge she had acquired, Anna staggered home, took a stiff drink, fried up some eggs and bacon, and went to bed.

'I'll call for you at eight o'clock tomorrow morning,' Liz had said. 'And for God's sake be ready.' Anna was ready. And from then on she was hooked.

It was as simple as that.

All she'd needed right from the beginning was a good hard job of work to do, and plenty of problems to solve — other people's problems instead of her own.

The work was arduous and often quite shattering emotionally, but Anna was absorbed by every moment of it, and within about — we are skipping right forward now — within about a year and a half, she began to feel moderately happy once again. She was finding it more and more difficult to picture her husband vividly, to see him precisely as he was when he ran up the stairs to meet her, or when he sat across from her at supper in the evenings. The exact sound of his voice was becoming less easy to recall, and even the face itself, unless she glanced at a photograph, was no longer sharply etched in the memory. She still thought about him constantly, but she discovered that she could do so now without bursting into tears, and when she looked back on the way she had behaved a while ago, she felt slightly embarrassed. She started taking a mild interest in her clothes and in her hair, she returned to using lipstick and to shaving the hair from her legs. She enjoyed her food, and when people smiled at her, she smiled right back at them and meant it. In other words, she was back in the swim once again. She was pleased to be alive.

It was at this point that Anna had to go down to Dallas on office business.

Liz's office did not normally operate beyond state lines, but in this instance, a couple who had adopted a baby through the agency had subsequently moved away from New York and gone to live in Texas. Now, five months after the move, the wife had written to say that she no longer wanted to keep the child. Her husband, she announced, had died of a heart attack soon after they'd arrived in Texas. She herself had remarried almost at once, and her new husband 'found it impossible to adjust to an adopted baby . . . '

Now this was a serious situation, and quite apart from the welfare of the child itself, there were all manner of legal obligations involved.

Anna flew down to Dallas in a plane that left

New York very early, and she arrived before breakfast. After checking in at her hotel, she spent the next eight hours with the persons concerned in the affair, and by the time she had done all that could be done that day, it was around four thirty in the afternoon and she was utterly exhausted. She took a cab back to the hotel, and went up to her room. She called Liz on the phone to report the situation, then she undressed and soaked herself for a long time in a warm bath. Afterwards, she wrapped up in a towel and lay on the bed, smoking a cigarette.

Her efforts on behalf of the child had so far come to nothing. There had been two lawyers there who had treated her with absolute contempt. How she hated them. She detested their arrogance and their softly spoken hints that nothing she might do would make the slightest difference to their client. One of them kept his feet up on the table all the way through the discussion, and both of them had rolls of fat on their bellies, and the fat spilled out into their shirts like liquid and hung in huge folds over their belted trouser-tops.

Anna had visited Texas many times before in her life, but until now she had never gone there alone. Her visits had always been with Ed, keeping him company on business trips; and during those trips, he and she had often spoken about the Texans in general and about how difficult it was to like them. One could ignore their coarseness and their vulgarity. It wasn't that. But there was, it seemed, a quality of ruthlessness still surviving among these people,

114

something quite brutal, harsh, inexorable, that it was impossible to forgive. They had no bowels of compassion, no pity, no tenderness. The only so-called virtue they possessed — and this they paraded ostentatiously and endlessly to strangers — was a kind of professional benevolence. It was plastered all over them. Their voices, their smiles, were rich and syrupy with it. But it left Anna cold. It left her quite, quite cold inside.

'Why do they love acting so tough?' she used to ask.

'Because they're children,' Ed would answer. 'They're dangerous children who go about trying to imitate their grandfathers. Their grandfathers *were* pioneers. These people aren't.'

It seemed that they lived, these present-day Texans, by a sort of egotistic will, push and be pushed. Everybody was pushing. Everybody was being pushed. And it was all very fine for a stranger in their midst to step aside and announce firmly, 'I will *not* push, and I will *not* be pushed.' That was impossible. It was especially impossible in Dallas. Of all the cities in the state, Dallas was the one that had always disturbed Anna the most. It was such a godless city, she thought, such a rapacious, gripped, iron, godless city. It was a place that had run amok with its money, and no amount of gloss and phony culture and syrupy talk could hide the fact that the great golden fruit was rotten inside.

Anna lay on the bed with her bath towel around her. She was alone in Dallas this time. There was no Ed with her now to envelop her in his incredible strength and love; and perhaps it was because of this that she began, all of a sudden, to feel slightly uneasy. She lit a second cigarette and waited for the uneasiness to pass. It didn't pass; it got worse. A hard little knot of fear was gathering itself in the top of her stomach, and there it stayed, growing bigger every minute. It was an unpleasant feeling, the kind one might experience if one were alone in the house at night and heard, or thought one heard, a footstep in the next room.

In this place there were a million footsteps, and she could hear them all.

She got off the bed and went over to the window, still wrapped in her towel. Her room was on the twenty-second floor, and the window was open. The great city lay pale and milky-yellow in the evening sunshine. The street below was solid with automobiles. The sidewalk was filled with people. Everybody was hustling home from work, pushing and being pushed. She felt the need of a friend. She wanted very badly to have someone to talk to at this moment. She would have liked a house to go to, a house with a family — a wife and husband and children and rooms full of toys, and the husband and wife would fling their arms around her at the front door and cry out, 'Anna! How marvellous to see you! How long can you stay? A week, a month, a year?'

All of a sudden, as so often happens in situations like this, her memory went *click*, and she said aloud, 'Conrad Kreuger! Good heavens above! *He* lives in Dallas . . . at least he used to . . . '

She hadn't seen Conrad since they were classmates in high school, in New York. They were both about seventeen then, and Conrad had been her beau, her love, her everything. For over a year they had gone around together, and each of them had sworn eternal loyalty to the other, with marriage in the near future. Then suddenly Ed Cooper had flashed into her life, and that, of course, had been the end of the romance with Conrad. But Conrad did not seem to have taken the break too badly. It certainly couldn't have *shattered* him, because not more than a month or two later he had started going strong with another girl in the class . . .

Now what was *her* name?

A big handsome bosomy girl she was, with flaming red hair and a peculiar name, a very old-fashioned name. What was it? Arabella? No, not Arabella. Ara- something, though. Araminty? Yes! Araminty it was! And what is more, within a year or so, Conrad Kreuger had married Araminty and had carried her back with him to Dallas, the place of his birth.

Anna went over to the bedside table and picked up the telephone directory.

Kreuger, Conrad P., M.D.

That was Conrad all right. He had always said he was going to be a doctor. The book gave an office number and a residence number.

Should she phone him?

Why not?

She glanced at her watch. It was five twenty. She lifted the receiver and gave the number of his office.

117

'Doctor Kreuger's surgery,' a girl's voice answered.

'Hello,' Anna said. 'Is Doctor Kreuger there?'

'The doctor is busy right now. May I ask who's calling?'

'Will you please tell him that Anna Greenwood telephoned him.'

'Who?'

'Anna Greenwood.'

'Yes, Miss Greenwood. Did you wish for an appointment?'

'No, thank you.'

'Is there something I can do for you?'

Anna gave the name of her hotel, and asked her to pass it on to Dr Kreuger.

'I'll be very glad to,' the secretary said. 'Good-bye, Miss Greenwood.'

'Good-bye,' Anna said. She wondered whether Dr Conrad P. Kreuger would remember her name after all these years. She believed he would. She lay back again on the bed and began trying to recall what Conrad himself used to look like. Extraordinarily handsome, that he was. Tall . . . lean . . . big-shouldered . . . with almost pure-black hair . . . and a marvellous face . . . a strong carved face like one of those Greek heroes, Perseus or Ulysses. Above all, though, he had been a very gentle boy, a serious, decent, quiet, gentle boy. He had never kissed her much — only when he said good-bye in the evenings. And he'd never gone in for necking, as all the others had. When he took her home from the movies on Saturday nights, he used to park his old Buick outside her house and sit there in the car beside her, just talking and talking about the future, his future and hers, and how he was going to go back to Dallas to become a famous doctor. His refusal to indulge in necking and all the nonsense that went with it had impressed her no end. He respects me, she used to say. He loves me. And she was probably right. In any event, he had been a nice man, a nice good man. And had it not been for the fact that Ed Cooper was a super-nice, super-good man, she was sure she would have married Conrad Kreuger.

The telephone rang. Anna lifted the receiver. 'Yes,' she said. 'Hello.'

'Anna Greenwood?'

'Conrad Kreuger!'

'My dear Anna! What a fantastic surprise. Good gracious me. After all these years.'

'It's a long time, isn't it.'

'It's a lifetime. Your voice sounds just the same.'

'So does yours.'

'What brings you to our fair city? Are you staying long?'

'No, I have to go back tomorrow. I hope you didn't mind my calling you.'

'Hell, no, Anna. I'm delighted. Are you all right?'

'Yes, I'm fine. I'm fine now. I had a bad time of it for a bit after Ed died . . . '

'What!'

'He was killed in an automobile two and a half years ago.'

'Oh gee, Anna, I *am* sorry. How terrible. I . . . I don't know what to say . . . '

'Don't say anything.'

'You're okay now?'

'I'm fine. Working like a slave.'

'That's the girl . . . '

'How's . . . how's Araminty?'

'Oh, she's fine.'

'Any children?'

'One,' he said. 'A boy. How about you?'

'I have three, two girls and a boy.'

'Well, well, what d'you know! Now listen, Anna . . . '

'I'm listening.'

'Why don't I run over to the hotel and buy you a drink? I'd like to do that. I'll bet you haven't changed one iota.'

'I look old, Conrad.'

'You're lying.'

'I feel old, too.'

'You want a good doctor?'

'Yes. I mean no. Of course I don't. I don't want any more doctors. All I need is . . . well . . . '

'Yes?'

'This place worries me, Conrad. I guess I need a friend. That's all I need.'

'You've got one. I have just one more patient to see, and then I'm free. I'll meet you down in the bar, the something room, I've forgotten what it's called, at six, in about half an hour. Will that suit you?'

'Yes,' she said. 'Of course. And . . . thank you, Conrad.' She replaced the receiver, then got up from the bed, and began to dress.

She felt mildly flustered. Not since Ed's death

had she been out and had a drink alone with a man. Dr Jacobs would be pleased when she told him about it on her return. He wouldn't congratulate her madly, but he would certainly be pleased. He'd say it was a step in the right direction, a beginning. She still went to him regularly, and now that she had gotten so much better, his oblique references had become far less oblique and he had more than once told her that her depressions and suicidal tendencies would never completely disappear until she had actually and physically 'replaced' Ed with another man.

'But it is impossible to replace a person one has loved to distraction,' Anna had said to him the last time he had brought up the subject. 'Heavens above, doctor, when Mrs Crummlin-Brown's parakeet died last month, her *parakeet*, mind you, not her husband, she was so shook up about it, she swore she'd never have another bird again!'

'Mrs Cooper,' Dr Jacobs had said, 'one doesn't normally have sexual intercourse with a parakeet.'

'Well . . . no . . . '

'That's why it doesn't have to be replaced. But when a husband dies, and the surviving wife is still an active and a healthy woman, she will invariably get a replacement within three years if she possibly can. And vice versa.'

Sex. It was about the only thing that sort of doctor ever thought about. He had sex on the brain.

By the time Anna had dressed and taken the elevator downstairs, it was ten minutes after six.

121

The moment she walked into the bar, a man stood up from one of the tables. It was Conrad. He must have been watching the door. He came across the floor to meet her. He was smiling nervously. Anna was smiling, too. One always does.

'Well, well,' he said. 'Well well well,' and she, expecting the usual peck on the cheek, inclined her face upward toward his own, still smiling. But she had forgotten how formal Conrad was. He simply took her hand in his and shook it — once. 'This *is* a surprise,' he said. 'Come and sit down.'

The room was the same as any other hotel drinking-room. It was lit by dim lights, and filled with many small tables. There was a saucer of peanuts on each table, and there were leather bench-seats all around the walls. The waiters were rigged out in white jackets and maroon pants. Conrad led her to a corner table, and they sat down facing each other. A waiter was standing over them at once.

'What will you have?' Conrad asked.

'Could I have a martini?'

'Of course. Vodka?'

'No, gin, please.'

'One gin martini,' he said to the waiter. 'No. Make it two. I've never been much of a drinker, Anna, as you probably remember, but I think this calls for a celebration.'

The waiter went away. Conrad leaned back in his chair and studied her carefully. 'You look pretty good,' he said.

'You look pretty good yourself, Conrad,' she

told him. And so he did. It was astonishing how little he had aged in twenty-five years. He was just as lean and handsome as he'd ever been — in fact, more so. His black hair was still black, his eye was clear, and he looked altogether like a man who was no more than thirty years old.

'You *are* older than me, aren't you?' he said.

'What sort of a question is that?' she said, laughing. 'Yes Conrad, I am exactly one year older than you. I'm forty-two.'

'I thought you were.' He was still studying her with the utmost care, his eyes travelling all over her face and neck and shoulders. Anna felt herself blushing.

'Are you an enormously successful doctor?' she asked. 'Are you the best in town?'

He cocked his head over to one side, right over, so that the ear almost touched the top of the shoulder. It was a mannerism that Anna had always liked. 'Successful?' he said. 'Any doctor can be successful these days in a big city — financially, I mean. But whether or not I am absolutely first rate at my job is another matter. I only hope and pray that I am.'

The drinks arrived and Conrad raised his glass and said, 'Welcome to Dallas, Anna. I'm so pleased you called me up. It's good to see you again.'

'It's good to see you, too, Conrad,' she said, speaking the truth.

He looked at her glass. She had taken a huge first gulp, and the glass was now half empty. 'You prefer gin to vodka?' he asked.

'I do,' she said, 'yes.'

'You ought to change over.'

'Why?'

'Gin is not good for females.'

'It's not?'

'It's very bad for them.'

'I'm sure it's just as bad for males,' she said.

'Actually, no. It isn't nearly so bad for males as it is for females.'

'Why is it bad for females?'

'It just is,' he said. 'It's the way they're built. What kind of work are you engaged in, Anna? And what brought you all the way down to Dallas? Tell me about you.'

'Why is gin bad for females?' she said, smiling at him.

He smiled back at her and shook his head, but he didn't answer.

'Go on,' she said.

'No, let's drop it.'

'You can't leave me up in the air like this,' she said. 'It's not fair.'

After a pause, he said, 'Well, if you really want to know, gin contains a certain amount of the oil which is squeezed out of juniper berries. They use it for flavouring.'

'What does it do?'

'Plenty.'

'Yes, but what?'

'Horrible things.'

'Conrad, don't be shy. I'm a big girl now.'

He was still the same old Conrad, she thought, still as diffident, as scrupulous, as shy as ever. For that she liked him. 'If this drink is really doing horrible things to me,' she said, 'then it is unkind of you not to tell me what those things are.'

Gently, he pinched the lobe of his left ear with the thumb and forefinger of his right hand. Then he said, 'Well, the truth of the matter is, Anna, oil of juniper has a direct inflammatory effect upon the uterus.'

'Now come on!'

'I'm not joking.'

'Mother's ruin,' Anna said. 'It's an old wives' tale.'

'I'm afraid not.'

'But you're talking about women who are pregnant.'

'I'm talking about all women, Anna.' He had stopped smiling now, and he was speaking quite seriously. He seemed to be concerned about her welfare.

'What do you specialize in?' she asked him. 'What kind of medicine? You haven't told me that.'

'Gynaecology and obstetrics.'

'Ah-ha!'

'Have you been drinking gin for many years?' he asked.

'Oh, about twenty,' Anna said.

'Heavily?'

'For heaven's sake, Conrad, stop worrying about my insides. I'd like another martini, please.'

'Of course.'

He called the waiter and said, 'One vodka martini.'

'No,' Anna said, 'gin.'

He sighed and shook his head and said, 'Nobody listens to her doctor these days.'

'You're not my doctor.'

'No,' he said. 'I'm your friend.'

'Let's talk about your wife,' Anna said. 'Is she still as beautiful as ever?'

He waited a few moments, then he said, 'Actually, we're divorced.'

'Oh, no!'

'Our marriage lasted for the grand total of two years. It was hard work to keep it going even that long.'

For some reason, Anna was profoundly shocked. 'But she was such a beautiful girl,' she said. 'What happened?'

'Everything happened, everything you could possibly think of that was bad.'

'And the child?'

'She got him. They always do.' He sounded very bitter. 'She took him back to New York. He comes to see me once a year, in the summer. He's twenty years old now. He's at Princeton.'

'Is he a fine boy?'

'He's a wonderful boy,' Conrad said. 'But I hardly know him. It isn't much fun.'

'And you never married again?'

'No, never. But that's enough about me. Let's talk about you.'

Slowly, gently, he began to draw her out on the subject of her health and the bad times she had gone through after Ed's death. She found she didn't mind talking to him about it, and she told him more or less the whole story.

'But what makes your doctor think you're not

126

completely cured?' he said. 'You don't look very suicidal to me.'

'I don't think I am. Except that sometimes, not often, mind you, but just occasionally, when I get depressed, I have the feeling that it wouldn't take such a hell of a big push to send me over the edge.'

'In what way?'

'I kind of start edging toward the bathroom cupboard.'

'What do you have in the bathroom cupboard?'

'Nothing very much. Just the ordinary equipment a girl has for shaving her legs.'

'I see.' Conrad studied her face for a few moments, then he said, 'Is that how you were feeling just now when you called me?'

'Not quite. But I'd been thinking about Ed. And that's always a bit dangerous.'

'I'm glad you called.'

'So am I,' she said.

Anna was getting to the end of her second martini. Conrad changed the subject and began talking about his practice. She was watching him rather than listening to him. He was so damned handsome it was impossible not to watch him. She put a cigarette between her lips, then offered the pack to Conrad.

'No thanks,' he said. 'I don't.' He picked up a book of matches from the table and gave her a light, then he blew out the match and said, 'Are those cigarettes mentholated?'

'Yes, they are.'

She took a deep drag, and blew the smoke

slowly up into the air. 'Now go ahead and tell me that they're going to shrivel up my entire reproductive system,' she said.

He laughed and shook his head.

'Then why did you ask?'

'Just curious, that's all.'

'You're lying. I can tell it from your face. You were about to give me the figures for the incidence of lung cancer in heavy smokers.'

'Lung cancer has nothing to do with menthol, Anna,' he said, and he smiled and took a tiny sip of his original martini, which he had so far hardly touched. He set the glass back carefully on the table. 'You still haven't told me what work you are doing,' he went on, 'or why you came to Dallas.'

'Tell me about menthol first. If it's even half as bad as the juice of the juniper berry, I think I ought to know about it quick.'

He laughed and shook his head.

'Please!'

'No, ma'am.'

'Conrad, you simply cannot start things up like this and then drop them. It's the second time in five minutes.'

'I don't want to be a medical bore,' he said.

'You're not being a bore. These things are fascinating. Come on! Tell! Don't be mean.'

It was pleasant to be sitting there feeling moderately high on two big martinis, and making easy talk with this graceful man, this quiet, comfortable, graceful person. He was not being coy. Far from it. He was simply being his normal scrupulous self.

'Is it something shocking?' she asked.

'No. You couldn't call it that.'

'Then go ahead.'

He picked up the packet of cigarettes still lying in front of her, and studied the label. 'The point is this,' he said. 'If you inhale menthol, you absorb it into the bloodstream. And that isn't good, Anna. It does things to you. It has certain very definite effects upon the central nervous system. Doctors still prescribe it occasionally.'

'I know that,' she said. 'Nose-drops and inhalations.'

'That's one of its minor uses. Do you know the other?'

'You rub it on the chest when you have a cold.'

'You can if you like, but it wouldn't help.'

'You put it in ointment and it heals cracked lips.'

'That's camphor.'

'So it is.'

He waited for her to have another guess.

'Go ahead and tell me,' she said.

'It may surprise you a bit.'

'I'm ready to be surprised.'

'Menthol,' Conrad said, 'is a well-known anti-aphrodisiac.'

'A what?'

'It suppresses sexual desire.'

'Conrad, you're making these things up.'

'I swear to you I'm not.'

'Who uses it?'

'Very few people nowadays. It has too strong a flavour. Saltpetre is much better.'

'Ah yes. I know about saltpetre.'

129

'What do you know about saltpetre?'

'They give it to prisoners,' Anna said. 'They sprinkle it on their cornflakes every morning to keep them quiet.'

'They also use it in cigarettes,' Conrad said.

'You mean prisoners' cigarettes?'

'I mean *all* cigarettes.'

'That's nonsense.'

'Is it?'

'Of course it is.'

'Why do you say that?'

'Nobody would stand for it,' she said.

'They stand for cancer.'

'That's quite different, Conrad. How do you know they put saltpetre in cigarettes?'

'Have you never wondered,' he said, 'what makes a cigarette go on burning when you lay it in the ashtray? Tobacco doesn't burn of its own accord. Any pipe smoker will tell you that.'

'They use special chemicals,' she said.

'Exactly; they use saltpetre.'

'Does saltpetre burn?'

'Sure it burns. It used to be one of the prime ingredients of old-fashioned gunpowder. Fuses, too. It makes very good fuses. That cigarette of yours is a first-rate slow-burning fuse, is it not?'

Anna looked at her cigarette. Though she hadn't drawn on it for a couple of minutes, it was still smouldering away and the smoke was curling upward from the tip in a slim blue-grey spiral.

'So this has menthol in it *and* saltpetre?' she said.

'Absolutely.'

'And they're *both* anti-aphrodisiacs?'

'Yes. You're getting a double dose.'

'It's ridiculous, Conrad. It's too little to make any difference.'

He smiled but didn't answer this.

'There's not enough there to inhibit a cockroach,' she said.

'That's what you think, Anna. How many do you smoke a day?'

'About thirty.'

'Well,' he said, 'I guess it's none of my business.' He paused, and then he added, 'But you and I would be a lot better off today if it was.'

'Was what?'

'My business.'

'Conrad, what *do* you mean?'

'I'm simply saying that if you, once upon a time, hadn't suddenly decided to drop me, none of this misery would have happened to either of us. We'd still be happily married to each other.'

His face had suddenly taken on a queer sharp look.

'Drop you?'

'It was quite a shock, Anna.'

'Oh dear,' she said, 'but everybody drops everybody else at that age, don't they?'

'I wouldn't know,' Conrad said.

'You're not cross with me still, are you, for doing that?'

'Cross!' he said. 'Good God, Anna! Cross is what children get when they lose a toy! I lost a wife!'

She stared at him, speechless.

131

'Tell me,' he went on, 'didn't you have any idea how I felt at the time?'

'But Conrad, we were so *young*.'

'It destroyed me, Anna. It just about destroyed me.'

'But how . . . '

'How what?'

'How, if it meant so much, could you turn right around and get engaged to somebody else a few weeks later?'

'Have you never heard of the rebound?' he asked.

She nodded, gazing at him in dismay.

'I was wildly in love with you, Anna.'

She didn't answer.

'I'm sorry,' he said. 'That was a silly outburst. Please forgive me.'

There was a long silence.

Conrad was leaning back in his chair, studying her from a distance. She took another cigarette from the pack, and lit it. Then she blew out the match and placed it carefully in the ashtray. When she glanced up again, he was still watching her. There was an intent, far look in his eyes.

'What are you thinking about?' she asked.

He didn't answer.

'Conrad,' she said, 'do you still hate me for doing what I did?'

'Hate you?'

'Yes, hate me. I have a queer feeling that you do. I'm sure you do, even after all these years.'

'Anna,' he said.

'Yes, Conrad?'

He hitched his chair closer to the table, and

leaned forward. 'Did it ever cross your mind . . . '

He stopped.

She waited.

He was looking so intensely earnest all of a sudden that she leaned forward herself.

'Did what cross my mind?' she asked.

'The fact that you and I . . . that both of us . . . have a bit of unfinished business.'

She stared at him.

He looked back at her, his eyes as bright as two stars. 'Don't be shocked,' he said, 'please.'

'Shocked?'

'You look as though I'd just asked you to jump out of the window with me.'

The room was full of people now, and it was very noisy. It was like being at a cocktail party. You had to shout to be heard.

Conrad's eyes waited on her, impatient, eager.

'I'd like another martini,' she said.

'Must you?'

'Yes,' she said, 'I must.'

In her whole life, she had been made love to by only one man — her husband, Ed.

And it had always been wonderful.

Three thousand times?

She thought more. Probably a good deal more. Who counts?

Assuming, though, for the sake of argument, that the exact figure (for there has to be an exact figure) was three thousand, six hundred and eighty . . .

. . . and knowing that every single time it happened it was an act of pure, passionate, authentic love-making between the same man and the same woman . . .

. . . then how in heaven's name could an entirely new man, an unloved stranger, hope to come in suddenly on the three thousand, six hundred and eighty-*first* time and be even halfway acceptable?

He'd be a trespasser.

All the memories would come rushing back. She would be lying there suffocated by memories.

She had raised this very point with Dr Jacobs during one of her sessions a few months back, and old Jacobs had said, 'There will be no nonsense about memories, my dear Mrs Cooper. I wish you would forget that. Only the present will exist.'

'But how do I get there?' she had said. 'How can I summon up enough nerve suddenly to go upstairs to a bedroom and take off my clothes in front of a new man, a stranger, in cold blood? . . . '

'Cold blood!' he had cried. 'Good God, woman, it'll be boiling hot!' And later he had said, 'Do at any rate try to believe me, Mrs Cooper, when I tell you that any woman who has been deprived of sexual congress after more than twenty years of practice — of uncommonly frequent practice in your case, if I understand you correctly — any woman in those circumstances is going to suffer continually from severe psychological disturbances until the routine is re-established. You are feeling a lot better, I know that, but it is my duty to inform you that you are by no means back to normal . . . '

To Conrad, Anna said, 'This isn't by any chance a therapeutic suggestion, is it?'

'A *what?*'

'A therapeutic suggestion.'

'What in the world do you mean?'

'It sounds exactly like a plot hatched up by my Dr Jacobs.'

'Look,' he said, and now he leaned right across the table and touched her left hand with the tip of one finger. 'When I knew you before, I was too damn young and nervous to make that sort of a proposition, much as I wanted to. I didn't think there was any particular hurry then, anyway. I figured we had a whole lifetime before us. I wasn't to know you were going to drop me.'

Her martini arrived. Anna picked it up and began to drink it fast. She knew exactly what it was going to do to her. It was going to make her float. A third martini always did that. Give her a third martini and within seconds her body would become completely weightless and she would go floating around the room like a wisp of hydrogen gas.

She sat there holding the glass with both hands as though it were a sacrament. She took another gulp. There was not much of it left now. Over the rim of her glass she could see Conrad watching her with disapproval as she drank. She smiled at him radiantly.

'You're not against the use of anaesthetics when you operate, are you?' she asked.

'Please, Anna, don't talk like that.'

'I am beginning to float,' she said.

135

'So I see,' he answered. 'Why don't you stop there?'

'What did you say?'

'I said, why don't you stop?'

'Do you want me to tell you why?'

'No,' he said. He made a little forward movement with his hands as though he were going to take her glass away from her, so she quickly put it to her lips and tipped it high, holding it there for a few seconds to allow the last drop to run out. When she looked at Conrad again, he was placing a ten-dollar bill on the waiter's tray, and the waiter was saying, 'Thank *you*, sir. Thank you indeed,' and the next thing she knew she was floating out of the room and across the lobby of the hotel with Conrad's hand cupped lightly under one of her elbows, steering her toward the elevators. They floated up to the twenty-second floor, and then along the corridor to the door of her bedroom. She fished the key out of her purse and unlocked the door and floated inside. Conrad followed, closing the door behind him. Then very suddenly, he grabbed hold of her and folded her up in his enormous arms and started kissing her with great gusto.

She let him do it.

He kissed her all over her mouth and cheeks and neck, taking deep breaths in between the kisses. She kept her eyes open, watching him in a queer detached sort of way, and the view she got reminded her vaguely of the blurry close-up view of a dentist's face when he is working on an upper back tooth.

Then all of a sudden, Conrad put his tongue

into one of her ears. The effect of this upon her was electric. It was as though a live two-hundred-volt plug had been pushed into an empty socket, and all the lights came on and the bones began to melt and the hot molten sap went running down into her limbs and she exploded into a frenzy. It was the kind of marvellous, wanton, reckless, flaming frenzy that Ed used to provoke in her so very often in the olden days by just a touch of the hand here and there. She flung her arms around Conrad's neck and started kissing him back with far more gusto than he had ever kissed her, and although he looked at first as though he thought she were going to swallow him alive, he soon recovered his balance.

Anna hadn't the faintest idea how long they stood there embracing and kissing with such violence, but it must have been for quite a while. She felt such happiness, such . . . such *confidence* again at last, such sudden over-whelming confidence in herself that she wanted to tear off her clothes and do a wild dance for Conrad in the middle of the room. But she did no such foolish thing. Instead, she simply floated away to the edge of the bed and sat down to catch her breath. Conrad quickly sat down beside her. She leaned her head against his chest and sat there glowing all over while he gently stroked her hair. Then she undid one button of his shirt and slid her hand inside and laid it against his chest. Through the ribs, she could feel the beating of his heart.

'What do I see here?' Conrad said.

'What do you see where, my darling?'

'On your scalp. You want to watch this, Anna.'

'You watch it for me, dearest.'

'Seriously,' he said, 'you know what this looks like? It looks like a tiny touch of androgenic alopecia.'

'Good.'

'No, it is not good. It's actually an inflammation of the hair follicles, and it causes baldness. It's quite common on women in their later years.'

'Oh, shut up, Conrad,' she said, kissing him on the side of the neck. 'I have the most gorgeous hair.'

She sat up and pulled off his jacket. Then she undid his tie and threw it across the room.

'There's a little hook on the back of my dress,' she said. 'Undo it, please.'

Conrad unhooked the hook, then unzipped the zipper and helped her to get out of the dress. She had on a rather nice pale-blue slip. Conrad was wearing an ordinary white shirt, as doctors do, but it was now open at the neck, and this suited him. His neck had a little ridge of sinewy muscle running up vertically on either side, and when he turned his head the muscle moved under the skin. It was the most beautiful neck Anna had ever seen.

'Let's do this very very slowly,' she said. 'Let's drive ourselves crazy with anticipation.'

His eyes rested a moment on her face, then travelled away, all the way down the length of her body, and she saw him smile.

'Shall we be very stylish and dissipated, Conrad, and order a bottle of champagne? I can ask room service to bring it up, and you can hide in the bathroom when they come in.'

'No,' he said. 'You've had enough to drink already. Stand up, please.'

The tone of his voice caused her to stand up at once.

'Come here,' he said.

She went close to him. He was still sitting on the bed, and now, without getting up, he reached forward and began to take off the rest of her clothes. He did this slowly and deliberately. His face had become suddenly rather pale.

'Oh, darling,' she said, 'how marvellous! You've got that famous thing! A real thick clump of hair growing out of each of your ears! You know what that means, don't you? It's *the* absolutely positive sign of enormous virility!' She bent down and kissed him on the ear. He went on taking off her clothes — the bra, the shoes, the girdle, the pants, and finally the stockings, all of which he dropped in a heap on the floor. The moment he had peeled off her last stocking and dropped it, he turned away. He turned right away from her as though she didn't exist, and now he began to undress himself.

It was rather odd to be standing so close to him in nothing but her own skin and him not even giving her a second look. But perhaps men did these things. Ed might have been an exception. How could *she* know? Conrad took off his white shirt first, and after folding it very carefully, he stood up and carried it to a chair and laid it on one of the arms. He did the same with his undershirt. Then he sat down again on the edge of the bed and started removing his shoes. Anna remained quite still, watching him. His sudden change of mood, his silence, his curious intensity, were making her a bit afraid. But they were also exciting her. There was a stealth, almost a menace in his movements, as though he were some splendid animal treading softly toward the kill. A leopard.

She became hypnotized watching him. She was watching his fingers, the surgeon's fingers, as they untied and loosened the laces of the left shoe, easing it off the foot, and placing it neatly half under the bed. The right shoe came next. Then the left sock and the right sock, both of them being folded together and laid with the utmost precision across the toes of the shoes. Finally the fingers moved up to the top of the trousers, where they undid one button and then began to manipulate the zipper. The trousers, when taken off, were folded along the creases, then carried over to the chair. The underpants followed.

Conrad, now naked, walked slowly back to the edge of the bed, and sat. Then at last, he turned his head and noticed her. She stood waiting . . . and trembling. He looked her slowly up and down. Then abruptly, he shot out a hand and took her by the wrist, and with a sharp pull he had her sprawled across the bed.

The relief was enormous. Anna flung her arms around him and held on to him tightly, oh so tightly, for fear that he might go away. She was in mortal fear that he might go away and not come back. And there they lay, she holding on to him as though he were the only thing left in the world to hold on to, and he, strangely quiet, watchful, intent, slowly disentangling himself and beginning to touch her now in a number of different places with those fingers of his, those expert surgeon's fingers. And once again she flew into a frenzy.

The things he did to her during the next few moments were terrible and exquisite. He was, she knew, merely getting her ready, preparing her, or as they say in the hospital, prepping her for the operation itself, but oh God, she had never known or experienced anything even remotely like this. And it was all exceedingly quick, for in what seemed to her no more than a few seconds, she had reached that excruciating point of no return where the whole room becomes compressed into a single tiny blinding speck of light that is going to explode and tear one to pieces at the slightest extra touch. At this stage, in a swift rapacious parabola, Conrad swung his body on top of her for the final act.

And now Anna felt her passion being drawn out of her as if a long live nerve were being drawn slowly out of her body, a long live thread of electric fire, and she cried out to Conrad to go on and on and on, and as she did so, in the middle of it all, somewhere above her, she heard another voice, and this other voice grew louder and louder, more and more insistent, demanding to be heard:

'I said are you *wearing* something?' the voice wanted to know.

'Oh darling, what is it?'

141

'I keep asking you, are you *wearing* something?'

'Who, me?'

'There's an obstruction here. You must be wearing a diaphragm or some other appliance.'

'Of course not, darling. Everything's wonderful. Oh, do be quiet.'

'Everything is *not* wonderful, Anna.'

Like a picture on a screen, the room swam back into focus. In the foreground was Conrad's face. It was suspended above her, on naked shoulders. The eyes were looking directly into hers. The mouth was still talking.

'If you're going to use a device, then for heaven's sake learn to introduce it in the proper manner. There is nothing so aggravating as careless positioning. The diaphragm has to be placed right back against the cervix.'

'But I'm not wearing anything!'

'You're not? Well, there's still an obstruction.'

Not only the room but the whole world as well seemed slowly to be sliding away from under her now.

'I feel sick,' she said.

'You what?'

'I feel sick.'

'Don't be childish, Anna.'

'Conrad, I'd like you to go, please. Go now.'

'What on earth are you talking about?'

'Go away from me, Conrad!'

'That's ridiculous, Anna. Okay, I'm sorry I spoke. Forget it.'

'Go away!' she cried. '*Go away! Go away! Go away!*'

She tried to push him away from her, but he was huge and strong and he had her pinned.

'Calm yourself,' he said. 'Relax. You can't suddenly change your mind like this, in the middle of everything. And for heaven's sake, don't start weeping.'

'Leave me alone, Conrad, I beg you.'

He seemed to be gripping her with everything he had, arms and elbows, hands and fingers, thighs and knees, ankles and feet. He was like a toad the way he gripped her. He was exactly like an enormous clinging toad, gripping and grasping and refusing to let go. She had seen a toad once doing precisely this. It was copulating with a frog on a stone beside a stream, and there it sat, motionless, repulsive, with an evil yellow gleam in its eye, gripping the frog with its two powerful front paws and refusing to let go . . .

'Now stop struggling, Anna. You're acting like a hysterical child. For God's sake, woman, what's eating you?'

'You're hurting me!' she cried.

'*Hurting* you?'

'It's hurting me terribly!'

She told him this only to get him away.

'You know why it's hurting?' he said.

'Conrad! Please!'

'Now wait a minute, Anna. Allow me to explain . . . '

'No!' she cried. 'I've had enough explaining!'

'My dear woman . . . '

'No!' She was struggling desperately to free herself, but he still had her pinned.

'The reason it hurts,' he went on, 'is that you

143

are not manufacturing any fluid. The mucosa is virtually dry . . . '

'Stop!'

'The actual name is senile atrophic vaginitis. It comes with age, Anna. That's why it's called *senile* vaginitis. There's not much one can do . . . '

At that point, she started to scream. The screams were not very loud, but they were screams nevertheless, terrible, agonized stricken screams, and after listening to them for a few seconds, Conrad, in a single graceful movement, suddenly rolled away from her and pushed her to one side with both hands. He pushed her with such force that she fell on to the floor.

She climbed slowly to her feet, and as she staggered into the bathroom, she was crying 'Ed! . . . Ed! . . . Ed! . . . ' in a queer supplicating voice. The door shut.

Conrad lay very still listening to the sounds that came from behind the door. At first, he heard only the sobbing of the woman, but a few seconds later, above the sobbing, he heard the sharp metallic click of a cupboard being opened. Instantly, he sat up and vaulted off the bed and began to dress himself with great speed. His clothes, so neatly folded, lay ready at hand, and it took him no more than a couple of minutes to put them on. When that was done, he crossed to the mirror and wiped the lipstick off his face with a handkerchief. He took a comb from his pocket and ran it through his fine black hair. He walked once round the bed to see if he had forgotten anything. and then, carefully, like a man who is tiptoeing from a room where a child is sleeping, he moved out into the corridor, closing the door softly behind him.

Bitch

I have so far released for publication only one episode from Uncle Oswald's diaries. It concerned, as some of you may remember, a carnal encounter between my uncle and a Syrian female leper in the Sinai Desert. Six years have gone by since its publication and nobody has yet come forward to make trouble. I am therefore encouraged to release a second episode from these curious pages. My lawyer has advised against it. He points out that some of the people concerned are still living and are easily recognizable. He says I will be sued mercilessly. Well, let them sue. I am proud of my uncle. He knew how life should be lived. In a preface to the first episode I said that Casanova's *Memoirs* read like a Parish Magazine beside Uncle Oswald's diaries, and that the great lover himself, when compared with my uncle, appears positively undersexed. I stand by that, and given time I shall prove it to the world. Here then is a little episode from Volume XXIII, precisely as Uncle Oswald wrote it:

PARIS
Wednesday
Breakfast at ten. I tried the honey. It was delivered yesterday in an early Sèvres sucrier which had that lovely canary-coloured ground known as *jonquille*. 'From Suzie,' the note said,

'and thank you.' It is nice to be appreciated. And the honey was interesting. Suzie Jolibois had, among other things, a small farm south of Casablanca, and was fond of bees. Her hives were set in the midst of a plantation of *cannabis indica*, and the bees drew their nectar exclusively from this source. They lived, those bees, in a state of perpetual euphoria and were disinclined to work. The honey was therefore very scarce. I spread a third piece of toast. The stuff was almost black. It had a pungent aroma. The telephone rang. I put the receiver to my ear and waited. I never speak first when called. After all, I'm not phoning them. They're phoning me.

'Oswald! Are you there?'

I knew the voice. 'Yes, Henri,' I said. 'Good morning.'

'Listen!' he said, speaking fast and sounding excited. 'I think I've got it! I'm almost certain I've got it! Forgive me if I'm out of breath, but I've just had a rather fantastic experience. It's all right now. Everything's fine. Will you come over?'

'Yes,' I said. 'I'll come over.' I replaced the receiver and poured myself another cup of coffee. Had Henri really done it at last? If he had, then I wanted to be around to share the fun.

I must pause here to tell you how I met Henri Biotte. Some three years ago I drove down to Provence to spend a summer weekend with a lady who was interesting to me simply because she possessed an extraordinarily powerful muscle in a region where other women have no muscles

147

at all. An hour after my arrival, I was strolling alone on the lawn beside the river when a small dark man approached me. He had black hairs on the backs of his hands and he made me a little bow and said, 'Henri Biotte, a fellow guest.'

'Oswald Cornelius,' I said.

Henri Biotte was as hairy as a goat. His chin and cheeks were covered with bristly black hair and thick tufts of it were sprouting from his nostrils. 'May I join you?' he said, falling into step beside me and starting immediately to talk. And what a talker he was! How Gallic, how excitable. He walked with a mad little hop, and his fingers flew as if he wanted to scatter them to the four winds of heaven, and his words went off like firecrackers, with terrific speed. He was a Belgian chemist, he said, working in Paris. He was an olfactory chemist. He had devoted his life to the study of olfaction.

'You mean smell?' I said.

'Yes, yes!' he cried. 'Exactly! I am an expert on smells. I know more about smells than anyone else in the world!'

'Good smells or bad?' I asked, trying to slow him down.

'Good smells, lovely smells, glorious smells!' he said. 'I make them! I can make any smell you want!'

He went on to tell me he was the chief perfume blender to one of the great couturiers in the city. And his nose, he said, placing a hairy finger on the tip of his hairy proboscis, probably looked just like any other nose, did it not? I wanted to tell him it had more hairs sprouting from the noseholes than wheat from the prairies and why didn't he get his barber to snip them out, but instead I confessed politely that I could see nothing unusual about it.

'Quite so,' he said. 'But in actual fact it is a smelling organ of phenomenal sensitivity. With two sniffs it can detect the presence of a single drop of macroylic musk in a gallon of geranium oil.'

'Extraordinary,' I said.

'On the Champs Elysées,' he went on, 'which is a wide thoroughfare, my nose can identify the precise perfume being used by a woman walking on the other side of the street.'

'With the traffic in between?'

'With heavy traffic in between,' he said.

He went on to name two of the most famous perfumes in the world, both of them made by the fashion-house he worked for. 'Those are my personal creations,' he said modestly. 'I blended them myself. They have made a fortune for the celebrated old bitch who runs the business.'

'But not for you?'

'Me! I am but a poor miserable employee on a salary,' he said, spreading his palms and hunching his shoulders so high they touched his earlobes. 'One day, though, I shall break away and pursue my dream.'

'You have a dream?'

'I have a glorious, tremendous, exciting dream, my dear sir!'

'Then why don't you pursue it?'

'Because first I must find a man farsighted enough and wealthy enough to back me.'

Ah-ha, I thought, so that's what it's all about. 'With a reputation like yours, that shouldn't be too difficult,' I said.

'The sort of rich man I seek is hard to find,' he said. 'He must be a sporty gambler with a very keen appetite for the bizarre.'

That's me, you clever little bugger, I thought. 'What is this dream you wish to pursue?' I asked him. 'Is it making perfumes?'

'My dear fellow!' he cried. 'Anyone can make *perfumes*! I'm talking about *the* perfume! The *only* one that counts!'

'Which would that be?'

'Why, the *dangerous* one, of course! And when I have made it, I shall rule the world!'

'Good for you,' I said.

'I am not joking, Monsieur Cornelius. Would you permit me to explain what I am driving at?'

'Go ahead.'

'Forgive me if I sit down,' he said, moving toward a bench. 'I had a heart attack last April and I have to be careful.'

'I'm sorry to hear that.'

'Oh, don't be sorry. All will be well so long as I don't overdo things.'

It was a lovely afternoon and the bench was on the lawn near the riverbank and we sat down on it. Beside us, the river flowed slow and smooth and deep, and there were little clouds of water-flies hovering over the surface. Across the river there were willows along the bank and beyond the willows an emerald-green meadow, yellow with buttercups, and a single cow grazing. The cow was brown and white.

'I will tell you what kind of perfume I wish to make,' he said. 'But it is essential I explain a few other things to you on the way or you will not fully understand. So please bear with me a while.' One hand lay limp upon his lap, the hairy part upward. It looked like a black rat. He was stroking it gently with the fingers of the other hand.

'Let us consider first,' he said, 'the phenomenon that occurs when a dog meets a bitch in heat. The dog's sexual drive is tremendous. All self-control disappears. He has only one thought in his head, which is to fornicate on the spot, and unless he is prevented by force, he will do so. But do you know what it is that causes this tremendous sex-drive in a dog?'

'Smell,' I said.

'Precisely, Monsieur Cornelius. Odorous molecules of a special conformation enter the dog's nostrils and stimulate his olfactory nerve-endings. This causes urgent signals to be sent to the olfactory bulb and thence to the higher brain centres. It is *all* done by smell. If you sever a dog's olfactory nerve, he will lose interest in sex. This is also true of many other mammals, but it is not true of man. Smell has nothing to do with the sexual appetite of the human male. He is stimulated in this respect by sight, by tactility, and by his lively imagination. Never by smell.'

'What about perfume?' I said.

'It's all rubbish!' he answered. 'All those expensive scents in small bottles, the ones I make, they have no aphrodisiac effect at all upon a man. Perfume was never intended for that purpose. In

151

the old days, women used it to conceal the fact that they stank. Today, when they no longer stink, they use it purely for narcissistic reasons. They enjoy putting it on and smelling their own good smells. Men hardly notice the stuff. I promise you that.'

'I do,' I said.

'Does it stir you physically?'

'No, not physically. Aesthetically, yes.'

'You enjoy the smell. So do I. But there are plenty of other smells I enjoy more — the bouquet of a good Lafite, the scent of a fresh Comice pear, or the smell of the air blowing in from the sea on the Brittany coast.'

A trout jumped high in midstream and the sunlight flashed on its body. 'You must forget,' said Monsieur Biotte, 'all the nonsense about musk and ambergris and the testicular secretions of the civet cat. We make our perfumes from chemicals these days. If I want a musky odour I will use ethylene sebacate. Phenylacetic acid will give me civet and benzaldehyde will provide the smell of almonds. No sir, I am no longer interested in mixing up chemicals to make pretty smells.'

For some minutes his nose had been running slightly, wetting the black hairs in his nostrils. He noticed it and produced a handkerchief and gave it a blow and a wipe. 'What I intend to do,' he said, 'is to produce a perfume which will have the same electrifying effect upon a man as the scent of a bitch in heat has upon a dog! One whiff and that'll be it! The man will lose all control. He'll rip off his pants and ravish the lady on the spot!'

'We could have some fun with that,' I said.

'We could rule the world!' he cried.

'Yes, but you told me just now that smell has nothing to do with the sexual appetite of the human male.'

'It doesn't,' he said. 'But it used to. I have evidence that in the period of the post-glacial drift, when primitive man was far more closely related to the ape than he is now, he still retained the ape-like characteristic of jumping on any right-smelling female he ran across. And later, in the Palaeolithic and Neolithic periods, he continued to become sexually animated by smell, but to a lesser and lesser degree. By the time the higher civilizations had come along in Egypt and China around 10,000 B.C., evolution had played its part and had completely suppressed man's ability to be stimulated sexually by smell. Am I boring you?'

'Not at all. But tell me, does that mean an actual physical change has taken place in man's smelling apparatus?'

'Absolutely not,' he said, 'otherwise there'd be nothing we could do about it. The little mechanism that enabled our ancestors to smell these subtle odours is still there. I happen to know it is. Listen, you've seen how some people can make their ears move a tiny bit?'

'I can do it myself,' I said, doing it.

'You see,' he said, 'the ear-moving muscle is still there. It's a leftover from the time when man used to be able to cock his ears forward for better hearing, like a dog. He lost that ability over a hundred thousand years ago, but the muscle remains. And the same applies to our smelling apparatus. The mechanism for smelling those secret smells is still there, but we have lost the ability to use it.'

'How can you be so certain it's still there?' I asked.

'Do you know how our smelling system works?' he said.

'Not really.'

'Then I shall tell you, otherwise I cannot answer your question. Attend closely, please. Air is sucked in through the nostrils and passes the three baffle-shaped turbinate bones in the upper part of the nose. There it gets warmer and filtered. This warm air now travels up and over two clefts that contain the smelling organs. These organs are patches of yellowish tissue, each about an inch square. In this tissue are embedded the nerve-fibres and nerve-endings of the olfactory nerve. Every nerve-ending consists of an olfactory cell bearing a cluster of tiny hair-like filaments. These filaments act as receivers. 'Receptors' is a better word. And when the receptors are tickled or stimulated by odorous molecules, they send signals to the brain. If, as you come downstairs in the morning, you sniff into your nostrils the odorous molecules of frying bacon, these will stimulate your receptors, the receptors will flash a signal along the olfactory nerve to the brain, and the brain will interpret it in terms of the character and intensity of the odour. And that is when you cry out, 'Ah-ha, bacon for breakfast!''

'I never eat bacon for breakfast,' I said.

He ignored this.

'These receptors,' he went on, 'these tiny hair-like filaments are what concern us. And now you are going to ask me how on earth they can tell the difference between one odorous molecule and another, between say peppermint and camphor?'

'How can they?' I said. I was interested in this.

'Attend more closely than ever now, please,' he said. 'At the end of each receptor is an indentation, a sort of cup, except that it isn't round. This is the 'receptor site'. Imagine now thousands of these little hair-like filaments with tiny cups at their extremities, all waving about like the tendrils of sea anemones and waiting to catch in their cups any odorous molecules that pass by. That, you see, is what actually happens. When you sniff a certain smell, the odorous molecules of the substance which made that smell go rushing around inside your nostrils and get caught by the little cups, the receptor sites. Now the important thing to remember is this. Molecules come in all shapes and sizes. Equally, the little cups or receptor sites are also differently shaped. Thus, the molecules lodge only in the receptor sites which fit them. Pepperminty molecules go only into special pepperminty receptor sites. Camphor molecules, which have a quite different shape, will fit only into the special camphor receptor sites, and so on. It's rather like those toys for small children where they have to fit variously shaped pieces into the right holes.'

'Let me see if I understand you,' I said. 'Are you saying that my brain will know it is a pepperminty smell simply because the molecule has lodged in a pepperminty reception site?'

155

'Precisely.'

'But you are surely not suggesting there are differently shaped receptor sites for every smell in the world?'

'No,' he said, 'as a matter of fact, man has only seven differently shaped sites.'

'Why only seven?'

'Because our sense of smell recognizes only seven 'pure primary odours'. All the rest are 'complex odours' made up by mixing the primaries.'

'Are you sure of that?'

'Positive. Our sense of taste has even less. It recognizes only four primaries — sweet, sour, salt, and bitter! All other tastes are mixtures of these.'

'What are the seven pure primary odours?' I asked him.

'Their names are of no importance to us,' he said. 'Why confuse the issue.'

'I'd like to hear them.'

'All right,' he said. 'They are camphoraceous, pungent, musky, ethereal, floral, pepperminty, and putrid. Don't look so sceptical, please. This isn't *my* discovery. Very learned scientists have worked on it for years. And their conclusions are quite accurate, *except in one respect.*'

'What's that?'

'*There is an eighth pure primary odour which they don't know about, and an eighth receptor site to receive the curiously shaped molecules of that odour!*'

'Ah-ha-ha!' I said. 'I see what you're driving at.'

'Yes,' he said, 'the eighth pure primary odour is the sexual stimulant that caused primitive man

156

to behave like a dog thousands of years ago. It has a very peculiar molecular structure.'

'Then you know what it is?'

'Of course I know what it is.'

'And you say we still retain the receptor sites for these peculiar molecules to fit into?'

'Absolutely.'

'This mysterious smell,' I said, 'does it ever reach our own nostrils nowadays?'

'Frequently.'

'Do we smell it? I mean, are we aware of it?'

'No.'

'You mean the molecules don't get caught in the receptor sites?'

'They do, my dear fellow, they do. But nothing happens. No signal is sent off to the brain. The telephone line is out of action. It's like that ear muscle. The mechanism is still there, but we've lost the ability to use it properly.'

'And what do you propose to do about that?' I asked.

'I shall reactivate it,' he said. 'We are dealing with nerves here, not muscles. And these nerves are not dead or injured, they're merely dormant. I shall probably increase the intensity of the smell a thousandfold, and add a catalyst.'

'Go on,' I said.

'That's enough.'

'I should like to hear more,' I said.

'Forgive me for saying so, Monsieur Cornelius, but I don't think you know enough about organoleptic quality to follow me any further. The lecture is over.'

Henri Biotte sat smug and quiet on the bench

beside the river stroking the back of one hand with the fingers of the other. The tufts of hair sprouting from his nostrils gave him a pixie look, but that was camouflage. He struck me rather as a dangerous and dainty little creature, someone who lurked behind stones with a sharp eye and a sting in his tail, waiting for the lone traveller to come by. Surreptitiously I searched his face. The mouth interested me. The lips had a magenta tinge, possibly something to do with his heart trouble. The lower lip was caruncular and pendulous. It bulged out in the middle like a purse, and could easily have served as a receptacle for small coins. The skin of the lip seemed to be blown up very tight, as though by air, and it was constantly wet, not from licking but from an excess of saliva in the mouth.

And there he sat, this Monsieur Henri Biotte, smiling a wicked little smile and waiting patiently for me to react. He was a totally amoral man, that much was clear, but then so was I. He was also a wicked man, and although I cannot in all honesty claim wickedness as one of my own virtues, I find it irresistible in others. A wicked man has a lustre all his own. Then again, there was something diabolically splendid about a person who wished to set back the sex habits of civilized man half a million years.

Yes, he had me hooked. So there and then, sitting beside the river in the garden of the lady from Provence, I made an offer to Henri. I suggested he should leave his present employment forthwith and set himself up in a small laboratory. I would pay all the bills for this little

158

venture as well as making good his salary. It would be a five-year contract, and we would go fifty-fifty on anything that came out of it.

Henri was ecstatic. 'You mean it?' he cried. 'You are serious?'

I held out my hand. He grasped it in both of his and shook it vigorously. It was like shaking hands with a yak. 'We shall control mankind!' he said. 'We'll be the gods of the earth!' He flung his arms around me and embraced me and kissed me first on one cheek, then on the other. Oh, this awful Gallic kissing. Henri's lower lip felt like the wet underbelly of a toad against my skin. 'Let's keep the celebrations until later,' I said, wiping myself dry with a linen handkerchief.

Henri Biotte made apologies and excuses to his hostess and rushed back to Paris that night. Within a week he had given up his old job and had rented three rooms to serve as a laboratory. These were on the third floor of a house on the Left Bank, on the Rue de Cassette, just off the Boulevard Raspaille. He spent a great deal of my money equipping the place with complicated apparatus, and he even installed a large cage into which he put two apes, a male and a female. He also took on an assistant, a clever and moderately presentable young lady called Jeanette. And with all that, he set to work.

You should understand that for me this little venture was of no great importance. I had plenty of other things to amuse me. I used to drop in on Henri maybe a couple of times a month to see how things were going, but otherwise I left him entirely to himself. My mind wasn't on his job. I hadn't the patience for that kind of research. And when results failed to come quickly, I began to lose all interest. Even the pair of over-sexed apes ceased to amuse me after a while.

Only once did I derive any pleasure from my visits to his laboratory. As you must know by now, I can seldom resist even a moderately presentable woman. And so, on a certain rainy Thursday afternoon, while Henri was busy applying electrodes to the olfactory organs of a frog in one room, I found myself applying something infinitely more agreeable to Jeanette in the other room. I had not, of course, expected anything out of the ordinary from this little frolic. I was acting more out of habit than anything else. But my goodness, what a surprise I got! Beneath her white overall, this rather austere research chemist turned out to be a sinewy and flexible female of immense dexterity. The experiments she performed, first with the oscillator, then with the high-speed centrifuge, were absolutely breathtaking. In fact, not since that Turkish tightrope walker in Ankara (see Vol. XXI) had I experienced anything quite like it. Which all goes to show for the thousandth time that women are as inscrutable as the ocean. You never know what you have under your keel, deep water or shallow, until you have heaved the lead.

I did not bother to visit the laboratory again after that. You know my rule. I never return to a female a second time. With me at any rate, women invariably pull out all the stops during the first encounter, and a second meeting can therefore be nothing more than the same old tune on the same old fiddle. Who wants that? Not me. So when I suddenly heard Henri's voice calling urgently to me over the telephone that morning at breakfast, I had almost forgotten his existence.

I drove through the fiendish Paris traffic to the Rue de Cassette. I parked the car and took the tiny elevator to the third floor. Henri opened the door of the laboratory. 'Don't move!' he cried. 'Stay right where you are!' He scuttled away and returned in a few seconds holding a little tray upon which lay two greasy-looking red rubber objects. 'Noseplugs,' he said. 'Put them in, please. Like me. Keep out the molecules. Go on, ram them in tight. You'll have to breathe through your mouth, but who cares?'

Each noseplug had a short length of blue string attached to its blunt lower end, presumably for pulling it back out of the nostril. I could see the two bits of blue string dangling from Henri's nostrils. I inserted my own noseplugs. Henri inspected them. He rammed them in tighter with his thumb. Then he went dancing back into the lab, waving his hairy hands and crying out, 'Come in now, my dear Oswald! Come in, come in! Forgive my excitement, but this is a great day for me!' The plugs in his nose made him speak as though he had a bad cold. He hopped over to a cupboard and reached inside. He brought out one of those small square bottles made of very thick glass that hold about an ounce of perfume. He carried it over to where I stood, cupping his hands around it as though it were a tiny bird. 'Look! Here it is! The most

161

precious fluid in the entire world!'

This is the sort of rubbishy overstatement I dislike intensely. 'So you think you've done it?' I said.

'I know I've done it, Oswald! I am certain I've done it!'

'Tell me what happened.'

'That's not so easy,' he said. 'But I can try.'

He placed the little bottle carefully on the bench. 'I had left this particular blend, Number 1076, to distil overnight,' he went on. 'That was because only one drop of distillate is produced every half hour. I had it dripping into a sealed beaker to prevent evaporation. All these fluids are extremely volatile. And so, soon after I arrived at eight thirty this morning, I went over to Number 1076 and lifted the seal from the beaker. I took a tiny sniff. Just one tiny sniff. Then I replaced the seal.'

'And then?'

'Oh, my God, Oswald, it was fantastic! I completely lost control of myself! I did things I would never in a million years have dreamed of doing!'

'Such as what?'

'My dear fellow, I went completely wild! I was like a wild beast, an animal! I was not human! The civilizing influences of centuries simply dropped away! I was Neolithic!'

'What did you do?'

'I can't remember the next bit very clearly. It was all so quick and violent. But I became overwhelmed by the most terrifying sensation of lust it is possible to imagine. Everything else was blotted out of my mind. All I wanted was a

162

woman. I felt that if I didn't get hold of a woman immediately, I would explode.'

'Lucky Jeanette,' I said, glancing toward the next room. 'How is she now?'

'Jeanette left me over a year ago,' he said. 'I replaced her with a brilliant young chemist called Simone Gautier.'

'Lucky Simone, then.'

'No, no!' Henri cried. 'That was the awful thing! She hadn't arrived! Today of all days, she was late for work! I began to go mad. I dashed out into the corridor and down the stairs. I was like a dangerous animal. I was hunting for a woman, any woman, and heaven help her when I found her!'

'And who did you find?'

'Nobody, thank God. Because suddenly, I regained my senses. The effect had worn off. It was very quick, and I was standing alone on the second-floor landing. I felt cold. But I knew at once exactly what had happened. I ran back upstairs and re-entered this room with my nostrils pinched tightly between finger and thumb. I went straight to the drawer where I stored the noseplugs. Ever since I started working on this project, I have kept a supply of noseplugs ready for just such an occasion. I rammed in the plugs. Now I was safe.'

'Can't the molecules get up into the nose through the mouth?' I asked him.

'They can't reach the receptor sites,' he said. 'That's why you can't smell through your mouth. So I went over to the apparatus and switched off the heat. I then transferred the tiny

163

quantity of precious fluid from the beaker to this very solid airtight bottle you see here. In it there are precisely eleven cubic centimetres of Number 1076.'

'Then you telephoned me.'

'Not immediately, no. Because at that point, Simone arrived. She took one look at me and ran into the next room, screaming.'

'Why did she do that?'

'My God, Oswald, I was standing there stark naked and I hadn't realized it. I must have ripped off all my clothes!'

'Then what?'

'I got dressed again. After that, I went and told Simone exactly what had happened. When she heard the truth, she became as excited as me. Don't forget, we've been working on this together for over a year now.'

'Is she still here?'

'Yes. She's next door in the other lab.'

It was quite a story Henri had told me. I picked up the little square bottle and held it against the light. Through the thick glass I could see about half an inch of fluid, pale and pinkish-grey, like the juice of a ripe quince.

'Don't drop it,' Henri said. 'Better put it down.' I put it down. 'The next step,' he went on, 'will be to make an accurate test under scientific conditions. For that I shall have to spray a measured quantity on to a woman and then let a man approach her. It will be necessary for me to observe the operation at close range.'

'You are a dirty old man,' I said.

'I am an olfactory chemist,' he said primly.

'Why don't I go out into the street with my noseplugs in,' I said, 'and spray some on to the first woman who comes along. You can watch from the window here. It ought to be fun.'

'It would be fun all right,' Henri said. 'But not very scientific. I must make the tests indoors under controlled conditions.'

'And I will play the male part,' I said.

'No, Oswald.'

'What do you mean, no. I insist.'

'Now listen to me,' Henri said. 'We have not yet found out what will happen when a woman is present. This stuff is very powerful, I am certain of that. And you, my dear sir, are not exactly young. It could be extremely dangerous. It could drive you beyond the limit of your endurance.'

I was stung. 'There are no limits to my endurance,' I said.

'Rubbish,' Henri said. 'I refuse to take chances. That is why I have engaged the fittest and strongest young man I could find.'

'You mean you've already done this?'

'Certainly I have,' Henri said. 'I am excited and impatient. I want to get on. The boy will be here any minute.'

'Who is he?'

'A professional boxer.'

'Good God.'

'His name is Pierre Lacaille. I am paying him one thousand francs for the job.'

'How did you find him?'

'I know a lot more people than you think, Oswald. I am not a hermit.'

'Does the man know what he's in for?'

'I have told him that he is to participate in a scientific experiment that has to do with the psychology of sex. The less he knows the better.'

'And the woman? Who will you use there?'

'Simone, of course,' Henri said. 'She is a scientist in her own right. She will be able to observe the reactions of the male even more closely than me.'

'That she will,' I said. 'Does she realize what might happen to her?'

'Very much so. And I had one hell of a job persuading her to do it. I had to point out that she would be participating in a demonstration that will go down in history. It will be talked about for hundreds of years.'

'Nonsense,' I said.

'My dear sir, through the centuries there are certain great epic moments of scientific discovery that are never forgotten. Like the time when Dr Horace Wells of Hartford, Connecticut, had a tooth pulled out in 1844.'

'What was so historic about that?'

'Dr Wells was a dentist who had been playing about with nitrous oxide gas. One day, he got a terrible toothache. He knew the tooth would have to come out, and he called in another dentist to do the job. But first he persuaded his colleague to put a mask over his face and turn on the nitrous oxide. He became unconscious and the tooth was extracted and he woke up again as fit as a flea. Now *that*, Oswald, was the first operation ever performed in the world under general anaesthesia. It started something big. We shall do the same.'

166

At this point, the doorbell rang. Henri grabbed a pair of noseplugs and carried them with him to the door. And there stood Pierre, the boxer. But Henri would not allow him to enter until the plugs were rammed firmly up his nostrils. I believe the fellow came thinking he was going to act in a blue film, but the business with the plugs must have quickly disillusioned him. Pierre Lacaille was a bantamweight, small, muscular, and wiry. He had a flat face and a bent nose. He was about twenty-two and not very bright.

Henri introduced me, then ushered us straight into the adjoining laboratory where Simone was working. She was standing by the lab bench in a white overall, writing something in a notebook. She looked up at us through thick glasses as we came in. The glasses had a white plastic frame.

'Simone,' Henri said, 'this is Pierre Lacaille.' Simone looked at the boxer but said nothing. Henri didn't bother to introduce me.

Simone was a slim thirtyish woman with a pleasant scrubbed face. Her hair was brushed back and plaited into a bun. This, together with the white spectacles, the white overall, and the white skin of her face, gave her a quaint antiseptic air. She looked as though she had been sterilized for thirty minutes in an autoclave and should be handled with rubber gloves. She gazed at the boxer with large brown eyes.

'Let's get going,' Henri said. 'Are you ready?'

'I don't know what's going to happen,' the boxer said. 'But I'm ready.' He did a little dance on his toes.

Henri was also ready. He had obviously

167

worked the whole thing out before I arrived. 'Simone will sit in that chair,' he said, pointing to a plain wooden chair set in the middle of the laboratory. 'And you, Pierre, will stand on the six-metre mark with your noseplugs still in.'

There were chalk lines on the floor indicating various distances from the chair, from half a metre up to six metres.

'I shall begin by spraying a small quantity of liquid on to the lady's neck,' Henri went on addressing the boxer. 'You will then remove your noseplugs and start walking slowly toward her.' To me he said, 'I wish first of all to discover the effective range, the exact distance he is from the subject when the molecules hit.'

'Does he start with his clothes on?' I asked.

'Exactly as he is now.'

'And is the lady expected to cooperate or to resist?'

'Neither. She must be a purely passive instrument in his hands.'

Simone was still looking at the boxer. I saw her slide the end of her tongue slowly over her lips.

'This perfume,' I said to Henri, 'does it have any effect upon a woman?'

'None whatsoever,' he said. 'That is why I am sending Simone out now to prepare the spray.' The girl went into the main laboratory, closing the door behind her.

'So you spray something on the girl and I walk toward her,' the boxer said. 'What happens then?'

'We shall have to wait and see,' Henri said. 'You are not worried, are you?'

'Me, worried?' the boxer said. 'About a woman?'

168

'Good boy,' Henri said. Henri was becoming very excited. He went hopping from one end of the room to the other, checking and rechecking the position of the chair on its chalk mark and moving all breakables such as glass beakers and bottles and test-tubes off the bench on to a high shelf. 'This isn't the ideal place,' he said, 'but we must make the best of it.' He tied a surgeon's mask over the lower part of his face, then handed one to me.

'Don't you trust the noseplugs?'

'It's just an extra precaution,' he said. 'Put it on.'

The girl returned carrying a tiny stainless-steel spray-gun. She gave the gun to Henri. Henri took a stop watch from his pocket. 'Get ready, please,' he said. 'You, Pierre, stand over there on the six-metre mark.' Pierre did so. The girl seated herself in the chair. It was a chair without arms. She sat very prim and upright in her spotless white overall with her hands folded on her lap, her knees together. Henri stationed himself behind the girl. I stood to one side. 'Are we ready?' Henri cried.

'Wait,' said the girl. It was the first word she had spoken. She stood up, removed her spectacles, placed them on a high shelf, then returned to her seat. She smoothed the white overall along her thighs, then clasped her hands together and laid them again on her lap.

'Are we ready now?' Henri said.

'Let her have it,' I said. 'Shoot.'

Henri aimed the little spray-gun at an area of bare skin just below Simone's ear. He pulled the

169

trigger. The gun made a soft hiss and a fine misty spray came out of its nozzle.

'Pull your noseplugs out!' Henri called to the boxer as he skipped quickly away from the girl and took up a position next to me. The boxer caught hold of the strings dangling from his nostrils and pulled. The vaselined plugs slid out smoothly.

'Come on, come on!' Henri shouted. 'Start moving! Drop the plugs on the floor and come forward slowly!' The boxer took a pace forward. 'Not so fast!' Henri cried. 'Slowly does it! That's better! Keep going! Keep going! Don't stop!' He was crazy with excitement, and I must admit I was getting a bit worked up myself. I glanced at the girl. She was crouching in the chair, just a few yards away from the boxer, tense, motionless, watching his every move, and I found myself thinking about a white female rat I had once seen in a cage with a huge python. The python was going to swallow the rat and the rat knew it, and the rat was crouching very low and still, hypnotized, transfixed, utterly fascinated by the slow advancing movements of the snake.

The boxer edged forward.

As he passed the five-metre mark, the girl unclasped her hands. She laid them palms downwards on her thighs. Then she changed her mind and placed them more or less underneath her buttocks, gripping the seat of the chair on either side, bracing herself, as it were, against the coming onslaught.

The boxer had just passed the two-metre mark when the smell hit him. He stopped dead. His eyes glazed and he swayed on his legs as though he had been tapped on the head with a mallet. I thought he was going to keel over, but he didn't. He stood there swaying gently from side to side like a drunk. Suddenly he started making noises through his nostrils, queer little snorts and grunts that reminded me of a pig sniffing around its trough. Then without any warning at all, he sprang at the girl. He ripped off her white overall, her dress, and her underclothes. After that, all hell broke loose.

There is little point in describing exactly what went on during the next few minutes. You can guess most of it anyway. I do have to admit, though, that Henri had probably been right in choosing an exceptionally fit and healthy young man. I hate to say it, but I doubt my middle-aged body could have stood up to the incredibly violent gymnastics the boxer seemed driven to perform. I am not a voyeur. I hate that sort of thing. But in this case, I stood there absolutely transfixed. The sheer animal ferocity of the man was frightening. He was like a wild beast. And right in the middle of it all, Henri did an interesting thing. He produced a revolver and rushed up to the boxer and shouted, 'Get away from that girl! Leave her alone or I'll shoot you!' The boxer ignored him, so Henri fired a shot just over the top of his head and yelled, 'I mean it, Pierre! I shall kill you if you don't stop!' The boxer didn't even look up.

Henri was hopping and dancing about the room and shouting, 'It's fantastic! It's magnificent! Unbelievable! It works! It works! We've done it, my dear Oswald! We've done it!'

The action stopped as quickly as it had begun. The boxer suddenly let go of the girl, stood up, blinked a few times, and then said, 'Where the hell am I? What happened?'

Simone, who seemed to have come through it all with no bones broken, jumped up, grabbed her clothes, and ran into the next room. 'Thank you, mademoiselle,' said Henri as she flew past him.

The interesting thing was that the bemused boxer hadn't the faintest idea what he had been doing. He stood there naked and covered with sweat, gazing around the room and trying to figure out how in the world he came to be in that condition.

'What did I do?' he asked. 'Where's the girl?'

'You were terrific!' Henri shouted, throwing him a towel. 'Don't worry about a thing! The thousand francs is all yours!'

Just then the door flew open and Simone, still naked, ran back into the lab. 'Spray me again!' she cried. 'Oh, Monsieur Henri, spray me just one more time!' Her face was alight, her eyes shining brilliantly.

'The experiment is over,' Henri said. 'Go away and dress yourself.' He took her firmly by the shoulders and pushed her back into the other room. Then he locked the door.

Half an hour later, Henri and I sat celebrating our success in a small café down the street. We were drinking coffee and brandy. 'How long did it go on?' I asked.

'Six minutes and thirty-two seconds,' Henri said.

I sipped my brandy and watched the people strolling by on the sidewalk. 'What's the next move?'

'First, I must write up my notes,' Henri said. 'Then we shall talk about the future.'

'Does anyone else know the formula?'

'Nobody.'

'What about Simone?'

'She doesn't know it.'

'Have you written it down?'

'Not so anyone else could understand it. I shall do that tomorrow.'

'Do it first thing,' I said. 'I'll want a copy. What shall we call the stuff? We need a name.'

'What do you suggest?'

'*Bitch*,' I said. 'Let's call it *Bitch*.' Henri smiled and nodded his head slowly. I ordered more brandy. 'It would be great stuff for stopping a riot,' I said. 'Much better than tear-gas. Imagine the scene if you sprayed it on an angry mob.'

'Nice,' Henri said. 'Very nice.'

'Another thing we could do, we could sell it to very fat, very rich women at fantastic prices.'

'We could do that,' Henri answered.

'Do you think it would cure loss of virility in men?' I asked him.

'Of course,' Henri said. 'Impotence would go out the window.'

'What about octogenarians?'

'Them, too,' he said, 'though it would kill them at the same time.'

'And marriages on the rocks?'

'My dear fellow,' Henri said. 'The possibilities are legion.'

173

At that precise moment, the seed of an idea came sneaking slowly into my mind. As you know, I have a passion for politics. And my strongest passion, although I am English, is for the politics of the United States of America. I have always thought it is over there, in that mighty and mixed-up nation, that the destinies of mankind must surely lie. And right now, there was a President in office whom I could not stand. He was an evil man who pursued evil policies. Worse than that, he was a humourless and unattractive creature. So why didn't I, Oswald Cornelius, remove him from office?

The idea appealed to me.

'How much *Bitch* have you got in the lab at the moment?' I asked.

'Exactly ten cubic centimetres,' Henri said.

'And how much is one dose?'

'We used one cc for our test.'

'That's all I want,' I said. 'One cc. I'll take it home with me today. And a set of noseplugs.'

'No,' Henri said. 'Let's not play around with it at this stage. It's too dangerous.'

'It is my property,' I said. 'Half of it is mine. Don't forget our agreement.'

In the end, he had to give in. But he hated doing it. We went back to the lab, inserted our noseplugs, and Henri measured out precisely one cc of *Bitch* into a small scent-bottle. He sealed the stopper with wax and gave me the bottle. 'I implore you to be discreet,' he said. 'This is probably the most important scientific discovery of the century, and it must not be treated as a joke.'

From Henri's place, I drove directly to the workshop of an old friend, Marcel Brossollet. Marcel was an inventor and manufacturer of tiny precise scientific gadgets. He did a lot of work for surgeons, devising new types of heart-valves and pacemakers and those little one-way valves that reduce intra-cranial pressure in hydrocephalics.

'I want you to make me,' I said to Marcel, 'a capsule that will hold exactly one cc of liquid. To this little capsule, there must be attached a timing device that will split the capsule and release the liquid at a predetermined moment. The entire thing must not be more than half an inch long and half an inch thick. The smaller the better. Can you manage that?'

'Very easily,' Marcel said. 'A thin plastic capsule, a tiny section of razor-blade to split the capsule, a spring to flip the razor-blade, and the usual pre-set alarm system on a very small ladies' watch. Should the capsule be fillable?'

'Yes. Make it so I myself can fill it and seal it up. Can I have it in a week?'

'Why not?' Marcel said. 'It is very simple.'

The next morning brought dismal news. That lecherous little slut Simone had apparently sprayed herself with the entire remaining stock of *Bitch*, over nine cubic centimetres of it, the moment she arrived at the lab! She had then sneaked up behind Henri, who was just settling himself at his desk to write up his notes.

I don't have to tell you what happened next. And worst of all, the silly girl had forgotten that Henri had a serious heart condition. Damn it, he wasn't even allowed to climb a flight of stairs. So when the molecules hit him the poor fellow didn't stand a chance. He was dead within a minute, killed in action as they say, and that was that.

The infernal woman might at least have waited until he had written down the formula. As it was, Henri left not a single note. I searched the lab after they had taken away his body, but I found nothing. So now more than ever, I was determined to make good use of the only remaining cubic centimetre of *Bitch* in the world.

A week later, I collected from Marcel Brossollet a beautiful little gadget. The timing device consisted of the smallest watch I had ever seen, and this, together with the capsule and all the other parts, had been secured to a tiny aluminium plate three eighths of an inch square. Marcel showed me how to fill and seal the capsule and set the timer. I thanked him and paid the bill.

As soon as possible, I travelled to New York. In Manhattan, I put up at the Plaza Hotel. I arrived there at about three in the afternoon. I took a bath, had a shave, and asked room service to send me up a bottle of Glenlivet and some ice. Feeling clean and comfortable in my dressing-gown, I poured myself a good strong drink of the delicious malt whisky, then settled down in a deep chair with the morning's *New York Times*. My suite overlooked Central Park, and through the open window I could hear the hum of traffic and the blaring of cab-drivers' horns on Central

Park South. Suddenly, one of the smaller headlines on the front page of the paper caught my eye. It said, PRESIDENT ON TV TONIGHT. I read on.

The President is expected to make an important foreign policy statement when he speaks tonight at the dinner to be given in his honour by the Daughters of the American Revolution in the ballroom of the Waldorf Astoria . . .

My God, what a piece of luck!
I had been prepared to wait in New York for many weeks before I got a chance like this. The President of the United States does not often appear with a bunch of women on television. And that was exactly how I had to have him. He was an extraordinarily slippery customer. He had fallen into many a sewer and had always come out smelling of shit. Yet he managed every time to convince the nation that the smell was coming from someone else, not him. So the way I figured it was this. A man who rapes a woman in full sight of twenty million viewers across the country would have a pretty hard time denying he ever did it.
I read on.

The President will speak for approximately twenty minutes, commencing at nine p.m. and all major TV networks will carry the speech. He will be introduced by Mrs Elvira Ponsonby, the incumbent President of the

Daughters of the American Revolution. When interviewed in her suite at the Waldorf Towers, Mrs Ponsonby said . . .

It was perfect! Mrs Ponsonby would be seated on the President's right. At ten past nine precisely, with the President well into his speech and half the population of the United States watching, a little capsule nestling secretly in the region of Mrs Ponsonby's bosom would be punctured and half a centimetre of *Bitch* would come oozing out on to her gilt lamé ball-gown. The President's head would come up, he would sniff and sniff again, his eyes would bulge, his nostrils would flare, and he would start snorting like a stallion. Then suddenly he would turn and grab hold of Mrs Ponsonby. She would be flung across the dining-table and the President would leap on top of her, with the pie à la mode and strawberry shortcake flying in all directions.

I leaned back and closed my eyes, savouring the delicious scene. I saw the headlines in the papers the next morning:

PRESIDENT'S BEST PERFORMANCE TO DATE
PRESIDENTIAL SECRETS REVEALED
TO NATION
PRESIDENT INAUGURATES BLUE TV

and so on.

He would be impeached the next day and I would slip quietly out of New York and head back to Paris. Come to think of it, I would be leaving tomorrow!

I checked the time. It was nearly four o'clock. I dressed myself without hurrying. I took the elevator down to the main lobby and strolled across to Madison Avenue. Somewhere around Sixty-second Street, I found a good florist's shop. There I bought a corsage of three massive orchid blooms all fastened together. The orchids were cattleyas, white and mauve splotches on them. They were particularly vulgar. So, undoubtedly, was Mrs Elvira Ponsonby. I had the shop pack them in a handsome box tied up with gold string. Then I strolled back to the Plaza, carrying the box, and went up to my suite.

I locked all doors leading to the corridor in case the maid should come in to turn back the bed. I got out the noseplugs and vaselined them carefully. I inserted them in my nostrils, ramming them home very hard. I tied a surgeon's mask over my lower face as an extra precaution, just as Henri had done. I was ready now for the next step.

With an ordinary nose-dropper, I transferred my precious cubic centimetre of *Bitch* from the scent bottle to the tiny capsule. The hand holding the dropper shook a little as I did this, but all went well. I sealed the capsule. After that, I wound up the tiny watch and set it to the correct time. It was three minutes after five o'clock. Lastly, I set the timer to go off and break the capsule at ten minutes past nine.

The stems of the three huge orchid blooms had been tied together by the florist with a broad one-inch-wide white ribbon and it was a simple matter for me to remove the ribbon and secure my little capsule and timer to the orchid stems with cotton thread. When that was done, I wound the ribbon back around the stems and over my gadget. Then I retied the bow. It was a nice job.

Next, I telephoned the Waldorf and learned that the dinner was to begin at eight o'clock, but that the guests must be assembled in the ballroom by seven thirty, before the President arrived.

At ten minutes to seven, I paid off my cab outside the Waldorf Towers entrance and walked into the building. I crossed the small lobby and placed my orchid box on the reception desk. I leaned over the desk, getting as close as possible to the clerk. 'I have to deliver this package to Mrs Elvira Ponsonby,' I whispered, using a slight American accent. 'It is a gift from the President.'

The clerk looked at me suspiciously.

'Mrs Ponsonby is introducing the President before he speaks tonight in the ballroom,' I added. 'The President wishes her to have this corsage right away.'

'Leave it here and I'll have it sent up to her suite,' the clerk said.

'No, you won't,' I told him. 'My orders are to deliver it in person. What's the number of her suite?'

The man was impressed. 'Mrs Ponsonby is in five-o-one,' he said.

I thanked him and went into the elevator. When I got out at the fifth floor and walked along the corridor, the elevator operator stayed and watched me. I rang the bell to five-o-one.

The door was opened by the most enormous

female I had ever seen in my life. I have seen giant women in circuses. I have seen lady wrestlers and weight-lifters. I have seen the huge Masai women in the plains below Kilimanjaro. But never had I seen a female so tall and broad and thick as this one. Nor so thoroughly repugnant. She was groomed and dressed for the greatest occasion of her life, and in the two seconds that elapsed before either of us spoke, I was able to take most of it in — the metallic silver-blue hair with every strand glued into place, the brown pig-eyes, the long sharp nose sniffing for trouble, the curled lips, the prognathous jaw, the powder, the mascara, the scarlet lipstick and, most shattering of all, the massive shored-up bosom that projected like a balcony in front of her. It stuck out so far it was a miracle she didn't topple forward with the weight of it all. And there she stood, this pneumatic giant, swathed from neck to ankles in the stars and stripes of the American flag.

'Mrs Elvira Ponsonby?' I murmured.

'I am Mrs Ponsonby,' she boomed. 'What do you want? I am extremely busy.'

'Mrs Ponsonby,' I said. 'The President has ordered me to deliver this to you in person.'

She melted immediately. 'The dear man!' she shouted. 'How perfectly gorgeous of him!' Two massive hands reached out to grab the box. I let her have it.

'My instructions are to make sure you open it before you go to the banquet,' I said.

'Sure I'll open it,' she said. 'Do I have to do it in front of you?'

'If you wouldn't mind.'

181

'Okay, come on in. But I don't have much time.'

I followed her into the living-room of the suite. 'I am to tell you,' I said, 'that it comes with all good wishes from one President to another.'

'Ha!' she roared. 'I like that! What a gorgeous man he is!' She untied the gold string of the box and lifted the lid. 'I guessed it!' she shouted. 'Orchids! How splendid! They're far grander than this poor little thing I'm wearing!'

I had been so dazzled by the galaxy of stars across her bosom that I hadn't noticed the single orchid pinned to the left-hand side.

'I must change over at once,' she said. 'The President will be expecting me to wear his gift.'

'He certainly will,' I said.

Now to give you an idea of how far her chest stuck out in front of her, I must tell you that when she reached forward to unpin the flower, she was only just able to touch it even with her arms fully extended. She fiddled around with the pin for quite a while, but she couldn't really see what she was doing and it wouldn't come undone. 'I'm terrified of tearing this gorgeous gown,' she said. 'Here, you do it.' She swung around and thrust her mammoth bust in my face. I hesitated. 'Go on!' she boomed. 'I don't have all night!' I went to it, and in the end I managed to get the pin unhooked from her dress.

'Now let's get the other one on,' she said.

I put aside the single orchid and lifted my own flowers carefully from the box.

'Have they got a pin?' she asked.

'I don't believe they have,' I said. That was something I'd forgotten.

'No matter,' she said. 'We'll use the old one.' She removed the safety-pin from the first orchid, and then, before I could stop her, she seized the three orchids I was holding and jabbed the pin hard into the white ribbon around the stems. She jabbed it almost exactly into the spot where my little capsule of *Bitch* was lying hidden. The pin struck something hard and wouldn't go through. She jabbed it again. Again it struck metal. 'What the hell's under here?' she snorted.

'Let me do it!' I cried, but it was too late, because the wet stain of *Bitch* from the punctured capsule was already spreading over the white ribbon and one hundredth of a second later the smell hit me. It caught me smack under the nose and it wasn't actually like a smell at all because a smell is something intangible. You cannot feel a smell. But this stuff was palpable. It was solid. It felt as though some kind of fiery liquid were being squirted up my nostrils under high pressure. It was exceedingly uncomfortable. I could feel it pushing higher and higher, penetrating far beyond the nasal passages, forcing its way up behind the forehead and reaching for the brain. Suddenly the stars and stripes on Mrs Ponsonby's dress began to wobble and bobble about and then the whole room started wobbling and I could hear my heart thumping in my head. It felt as though I were going under an anaesthetic.

At that point, I must have blacked out completely, if only for a couple of seconds.

When I came round again, I was standing naked in a rosy room and there was a funny feeling in my groin. I looked down and saw that my beloved sexual organ was three feet long and thick to match. It was still growing. It was lengthening and swelling at a tremendous rate. At the same time, my body was shrinking. Smaller and smaller shrank my body. Bigger and bigger grew my astonishing organ, and it went on growing, by God, until it had enveloped my entire body and absorbed it within itself. I was now a gigantic perpendicular penis, seven feet tall and as handsome as they come.

I did a little dance around the room to celebrate my splendid new condition. On the way I met a maiden in a star-spangled dress. She was very big as maidens go. I drew myself up to my full height and declaimed in a loud voice:

'The summer's flower is to the summer sweet,
It flourishes despite the summer's heat.
But tell me truly, did you ever see
A sexual organ quite so grand as me?'

The maiden leapt up and flung her arms as far around me as she could. Then cried out:

'Shall I compare thee to a summer's day?
Shall I . . . Oh dear, I know not what to say.
But all my life I've had an itch to kiss
A man who could erect himself like this.'

A moment later, the two of us were millions of miles up in outer space, flying through the universe in a shower of meteorites all red and gold. I was riding her bareback, crouching forward and gripping her tightly between my thighs. 'Faster!' I shouted, jabbing long spurs into her flanks. 'Go faster!' Faster and still faster she flew, spurting and spinning around the rim of the sky, her mane streaming with sun, and snow waving out of her tail. The sense of power I had was overwhelming. I was unassailable, supreme. I was the Lord of the Universe, scattering the planets and catching the stars in the palm of my hand and tossing them away as though they were ping-pong balls.

Oh, ecstasy and ravishment! Oh, Jericho and Tyre and Sidon! The walls came tumbling down and the firmament disintegrated, and out of the smoke and fire of the explosion, the sitting-room in the Waldorf Towers came swimming slowly back into my consciousness like a rainy day. The place was a shambles. A tornado would have done less damage. My clothes were on the floor. I started dressing myself very quickly. I did it in about thirty seconds flat. And as I ran toward the door, I heard a voice that seemed to be coming from somewhere behind an upturned table in the far corner of the room. 'I don't know who you are, young man,' it said. 'But you've certainly done me a power of good.'

We do hope that you have enjoyed reading
this large print book.

Did you know that all of our titles
are available for purchase?

We publish a wide range of high quality
large print books including:
Romances, Mysteries, Classics
General Fiction
Non Fiction and Westerns

Special interest titles available in
large print are:
The Little Oxford Dictionary
Music Book
Song Book
Hymn Book
Service Book

Also available from us courtesy of
Oxford University Press:
Young Readers' Dictionary
(large print edition)
Young Readers' Thesaurus
(large print edition)

For further information or a free
brochure, please contact us at:
Ulverscroft Large Print Books Ltd.,
The Green, Bradgate Road, Anstey,
Leicester, LE7 7FU, England.
Tel: (00 44) 0116 236 4325
Fax: (00 44) 0116 234 0205

SOMEONE LIKE YOU

Roald Dahl

As a ship crosses the ocean, one passenger hits on a seemingly foolproof way to win the gambling pool on its daily progress. Attendants at a gallery are presented with an incredible piece of art tattooed on the back of an old man. Three men are pitted against a venomous krait in an agonisingly tense battle of wits. Machines are invented that can write entire novels with the barest human input — or pick up the shrieks of roses when they are cut. And a small boy's game of spotting snakes in a carpet pattern transforms into something grotesquely, horrifyingly real . . .

KISS KISS

Roald Dahl

By pawning a fine mink coat, an unfaithful wife schemes to pull the wool over her husband's eyes. Tucked away in a rural cottage, a priceless piece of antique furniture is the subject of a deceptive bargain. In London, a young businessman thinks he has found a perfect room to let, despite the dottiness of its landlady. Sickly and frail, a beekeeper's baby daughter begins to thrive after her father employs his own special methods of feeding. And when a widow reads her late husband's final letter to her, she discovers he is still very much with her after death . . .

THE WONDERFUL STORY OF HENRY SUGAR

Roald Dahl

As fishermen drag a giant sea turtle onto a Jamaican beach, a crowd of tourists lays bids for its meat and shell — until a boy who can talk to animals begs for the creature's freedom. A driver stops to pick up a hitch-hiker — and finds that his passenger is a man of surprising talents. When his plough strikes a hard object, a farm labourer stops and investigates — only to discover a fabulous hoard of buried treasure beneath the soil. And an idle gambler trains himself to see through the backs of playing-cards — then sets off to the casinos . . .